HEY, HMONG GIRL,
WHASSUP?

The Journal of Choua Vang

| Leah Rempel |

Hamline University Press
Saint Paul, Minnesota
2004

Dedication

This book is for my ESL students: Chou, Christina, Mai Chou, Pa, Pang, Pa Nhia, Patience, Vilai, and in fond memory of Hue. Without their encouragement, enthusiasm, and suggestions this book would never have happened. Also, I thank them for providing the illustrations we were able to use throughout the book.

Hamline University
1536 Hewitt Avenue
Saint Paul, Minnesota 55104-1284
Copyright © 2004 by Hamline University. All rights reserved.
ISBN 0-9723721-5-6
Library of Congress Control Number 2004113537

Book editing, design, layout, and production management by Carr Creatives
First printing 2004
Printed in U.S.A.

PREFACE

As an ESL teacher I look for literature for my students that matches their reading levels, their interests, and whenever possible, reflects their experiences. Meeting all of those criteria all of the time is difficult. In my experience teaching urban Hmong youth it is not so difficult to find literature that they are interested in, but it is nearly impossible to find literature that reflects their experience. This was my goal in writing this book. This is a work of fiction, however, and any resemblance to real people is coincidental.

I believe that this is the first novel ever written specifically for Hmong teenagers, addressing issues that are unique to them. It is written at a reading level appropriate for ESL high school students yet it doesn't talk down to them—it uses language that is familiar to their lexicon.

It is also authentic. I workshopped this novel, chapter by chapter, with my Hmong ESL students. They conscientiously verified the experiences, language, and background of the story. Their life stories became interwoven with the characters in my book. I also interviewed various members of the Hmong community, both teenagers and adults, in order to assure the authenticity of the work. Several Hmong friends also read the book and made further suggestions.

Hey, Hmong Girl, Whassup? is a product of my master's thesis at Hamline University Graduate School of Education. Part of my research was to determine whether it was appropriate for a person to write fiction about a culture other than his or her own. In the end, my research concluded that only under circumstances where a writer has close contact with the community/culture, does extensive research, and interviews, workshops, and edits the book with members of that community is it appropriate.

This novel came out of that research. My professors at Hamline and others suggested I publish this portion of my thesis, along with a study guide for the classroom, as a means to open the dialogue and trigger class-room activities and discussions that could be transformative for both Hmong and non-Hmong students alike. I hope that it is an enjoyable, compelling read for students and teachers.

Saint Paul, Minnesota   L.R.
July 2004

TABLE OF CONTENTS

Introduction

Ms. Martinez, my creative writing teacher, told me my life was really interesting and that I should write it down like a journal. I used to keep a journal, but it just said stuff like how boring school was and what boys I had crushes on. When I look at it now, it seems kind of stupid.

The journal you're going to read is different than anything I've ever done before. Ms. Martinez said I could do it as a project for her class and get credit for it. I wrote about what happened in my life over the last several months, and now we're making it into a book that other kids in her classes can read next year. I'm kind of scared about sharing all my private thoughts with other kids, but it's exciting too. I'm changing all the names and some details so nobody will know it's about me unless I want them to. Even though I still keep a journal, the part you're going to read is only from November to April because a lot happened in those few months.

A lot of kids can't imagine a Hmong kid writing a book. They think Hmong kids are stupid because they go to the ESL classroom for extra help and they don't talk English perfectly. Actually, I don't have to go anymore. I guess my English is good enough now, but I still feel dumb sometimes.

Ms. Martinez says Hmong kids aren't stupid at all. She says it's just that we grew up speaking another language, and that we have a lot of catching up to do. She says we're lucky because we can speak two languages and most kids can only speak one. She should know because she grew up speaking Spanish. She moved here from Mexico when she was in elementary school. She has a little bit of an accent, but I think her English is just about perfect. How else could she be a creative writing teacher?

Most Hmong kids I know talk pretty good, but they have some problems in school, and they don't like to write because they hate making mistakes. I don't care. I know I can fix them later. When I write, all of my feelings escape through my fingers. I know some people take pills to help them relax, but my writing is that pill for me.

I think Hmong kids have a lot of stress in their lives so we need to find ways to chill out. For example, kids call us Hmong a lot of nasty names that I won't repeat here. Ms. Martinez is helping me edit this and I don't think she would want me to write those kinds of words. But kids on the bus are always threatening to beat us up. They say stuff like, "Go back to your own country, you ***ing Chinese." They're the ones who are stupid! I can't believe that some people think all Asians are Chinese. Also, this is my country. I was born here. What makes it more their country than my country?

It's not just kids who are mean, either. One time I was in Target with my family and this white woman wearing way too much make-up marched up to my mom and said, "Why don't you get off welfare and stop spitting out so many babies?" That really pissed me off. We're not on welfare, and people can have as many kids as they want. There's no law! Sometimes I feel embarrassed that there are so many kids in our family. I have eight brothers and sisters and I'm in the middle. Two of them are married and don't live with us anymore. Thank God. The house is too crowded already. We can hardly fit in our van unless a bunch of us sit on the floor in the back. But it's nobody's business but our own!

When people say nasty things like that, I feel like a tiny little bug getting squished. I try to ignore it, but it's hard. I don't understand why people have to be so mean.

A Little Bit About My Family and Culture

Before you read , I think you should know a little bit about my family. My father is a very traditional Hmong man. He thinks we should still live the way we did in Laos: the men should be in charge and the women should take orders and never question.

My mom started asking a lot of questions after they moved to America. She began by asking "Why do I have to keep having babies? We don't have a farm to take care of anymore so we don't need all the extra help." (My father says it's an honor to have children, and she's had four more kids since she asked that question.)

Last year she asked, "Why can't I take English lessons?" (Now she takes classes twice a week, but my father doesn't like it.)

Her latest question is, "Why do our daughters need to get married so young?" (Two of my older sisters got married when they were still in high school.) That question is a big part of my story.

If you saw my mother in a store you would probably think, "Oh, there's another old Hmong woman." She's only 41, but she looks older because her back is hunched over from so many years of hard work on the farm, and because she wears baggy dresses and aprons from the thrift store. She always wears flip flops whether it's summer or winter.

When she opens her mouth to speak English, she misses endings and important words. She sounds like a little bird twittering. It's hard to understand her unless you listen closely. Most people don't bother. I used to be embarrassed by her, but I'm not anymore. That's because this year she really showed me how much she cares, and that she'll do anything to help me.

My dad has problems with how my mom has changed. He doesn't like it that she sews shirts at a factory all day and then squeezes in

English lessons at night. He tells her in Hmong (they never speak English with each other), "This isn't your country. Someday we'll go back to Laos. You don't need to learn English or the American ways. I've already had to do that and your children are doing that. You must stay Hmong. Don't turn into an American woman." Even though he's had to change so he can fit in, he really hates it. He wants things to be the same as they were in Laos. That's why he's so strict with us kids and he tries to boss my mom around so much.

These days my mom stands up to my dad, but not in the way some women might. She bows her head and nods, but then she just keeps on doing what she thinks she has to to make a better life for our family. They both really love us kids, but they have such different ideas about what is best for us. You'll read all about that in my journal.

Oops, I forgot to introduce myself. My name is Choua Vang, and I am in tenth grade at Como High. I live in Frogtown, Saint Paul, Minnesota. A lot of Hmong people live in my neighborhood so I feel okay here even though it's not very safe. There are gangs and drugs and other dangerous stuff. My parents don't like me to go out after dark, but sometimes I sneak out anyway. I'm trying to be a good girl now because I got myself into a lot of trouble last year. I just want to be a normal kid doing normal kid things. But that's hard for Hmong kids, especially if you're a girl.

We live in a medium-sized green house on Sherburne Street. It has a front porch and the paint is peeling off. I like to pick at it in the summer. Up until recently, I shared a room with three of my sisters, but now just two. They get on my nerves a lot. Ka, my sister in eighth grade, is always stealing my clothes. Nou, my sister in third grade, always leaves her Barbies and junk all over the place. Mai is a year older than me. She doesn't share a room with us anymore, but when she did, she was hardly ever around. She went cruising and hung out with her friends all the time. Sometimes she didn't come home at night. She made me promise never to tell, and I didn't for a long, long time.

I think a lot of people don't understand why we Hmong folks live in America. They think we're here to collect welfare and take away white people's jobs. That's not true at all. I hate it that people are so stupid and don't know anything about us, but they still feel like they can judge us.

My mom and dad were born in Laos. That's where most Hmong people come from. Laos isn't at all like America. Hmong didn't live in apartments or houses or cities like they do here. They were farmers in the mountains, living in huts made out of bamboo or wood. They raised animals, vegetables and other crops that they could sell and eat. There were no grocery stores like Cub where they could run to and pick up a frozen pizza on their way home from work. There were no paychecks either. They just survived on what they could grow and sell.

Most of them had to walk miles through the hot, sweaty jungle every day to get to the area where they farmed. The kids didn't usually go to school. They helped on the farm instead. They got up before the sun came up and worked until it got dark.

I can't really imagine what it was like because it's so different from America, but I hear the stories all the time so I have an idea. It seems like it must have been a really hard life, and kind of boring too. I like watching MTV, talking on the phone with my friends and listening to my CDs. I also like it when my friends and I get to go to the Mall of America or to Walgreens to try on make-up. They couldn't do stuff like that in Laos.

In the 1970s, there was this big war in Asia, and for some reason the Americans were part of it. I don't really understand why because Laos is halfway around the world from here. Anyway, the Americans asked the Hmong people to help fight this war. Hmong men were trained as pilots and soldiers, and they risked their lives in the air and in the jungle, fighting for the Americans. A lot of them died. When the Americans lost the war, the winners, called Communists, started killing the Hmong people because they had helped the Americans, not them. Hundreds of thousands of Hmong were killed. Both of my grandpas were killed and a bunch of my uncles. I never met any of them because I wasn't born yet.

The Hmong people had to run away and leave everything behind. People walked for hundreds of miles, hiding from Communist soldiers. Lots of them were caught and killed or starved to death.

Sometimes my dad tells the story about his brother's family. While they were escaping through the jungle, they spotted some Communist soldiers who were hunting down the Hmong. They quickly hid behind some trees, but their little baby started to cry. They knew they'd be killed if they were caught so my aunt put her hand over the baby's mouth really hard so the soldiers wouldn't hear him crying. They weren't caught, but when my aunt took her hand off the baby's mouth, he was dead. He couldn't breathe. There were a lot of parents who gave their babies opium while they were running away because it put them to sleep and kept them quiet. The horrible thing is, a lot of babies died because their parents accidentally gave them too much. I could tell you sad stories all day about all the awful stuff that happened to the Hmong.

The people who got through the jungle without getting caught crossed a big river called the Mekong to get to Thailand. They heard they would be safe in that country. Mostly they tried to cross at night. A lot of them floated across on inner tubes or built rafts from banana trees from the jungle. Sometimes they paid a lot of money to rent canoes, and then they were killed by those same people. Then they took all their money and belongings. Sometimes soldiers hid in the bushes beside the river and waited until they were in the water and then they'd shoot them when they were crossing. A whole lot of people drowned, too. The Mekong River isn't just a little stream that you can wade across. It is a big wide river with strong currents, and it's deep too.

Many Hmong actually made it to Thailand, but a lot of people were raped, robbed or killed once they got there. The ones who survived asked the government for protection. The Thai government didn't know what to do with so many extra people. They built these huge towns with walls around them. They were called refugee camps. The Hmong people were trapped there until the government decided what to do with them. There wasn't enough food, there was no running water, and they were really crowded and uncomfortable. The Hmong didn't have their farms to make a living anymore, and they weren't allowed to leave the refugee camps. It was like a prison only they hadn't done anything wrong. Even so, I think a lot of people liked living there because they felt safe, and the kids could run around without their parents having to worry about them.

I have two sisters who were born in Laos, and a brother and sister who were born at the refugee camp in Thailand. After waiting there six years, my family's application was finally accepted to come to America. Our cousins sponsored us. They came to Minnesota the year before we did.

So now you can see that the reason we live in America is because the Hmong sacrificed their lives to help this country, and the government owes us. Our whole culture was almost destroyed because of the war we helped fight. That's why it makes me so angry when people say we're just trying to take advantage by coming here.

I was born here in St. Paul. I think it's harder for my brothers and sisters who weren't born here to learn English because they never heard any when they were little. I knew a little bit of English before I started school because I went to Head Start. Now I understand almost everything except for really big words and some stuff in social studies and science classes. It's also kind of hard when teachers talk really fast and they never stop to explain anything. I think Ms. Martinez, my creative writing teacher, remembers what it was like not understanding everything because she doesn't talk too fast, and she always explains things very clearly and repeats her directions. That helps me a lot.

So anyway, my family moved here in 1985. That was 15 years ago. I was born a few months after they arrived. That means my mom was pregnant with me in Thailand. It's kind of cool that I've been to Asia even though I don't remember it. Sometimes my mom tells me about how scared she was when she went to the hospital when it was time for me to be born. Before me, all of my brothers and sisters were born at home. I think my mom just bent down and pushed and pushed, and the kids popped out. She said it was no big deal. Now that they were in America, my mother was told that she had to go to the hospital to have a baby because it wasn't safe to have kids at home.

At the hospital, a doctor hooked her up to all sorts of machines and tubes, made her take off her clothes and he examined her private parts. She was so embarrassed and she didn't understand anything he was saying. At first she thought he was trying to hurt her, but a very nice nurse held her hand and sang to her while I was being born so that helped.

Now my mom is afraid of hospitals. Until this year, even when one of us kids got really sick, she hardly ever took us to a doctor. Instead, she called a shaman who is a Hmong kind of spiritual healer, and he came to our house and did some kind of magic to make us better. I don't really get it, but it usually works. If one of us is really sick, sometimes we might have to kill a chicken or pig at the Hmong slaughterhouse or in the garage as an offering to the gods. If you're not Hmong, I don't expect you to understand it, but I also don't think you should make fun of it. Some people say we kill dogs and eat them, but that's just not true.

I've told you enough about my family and our culture. Now you can read. I hope you like it, and if you're not Hmong, I hope it helps you understand Hmong kids a little better.

My Journal

Thursday, November 2

In Hmong culture, girls often get married really young. Back in Laos, some girls got married when they were eleven or twelve. In America, they wait a little bit longer, but two of my older sisters got married when they were fifteen and sixteen years old. They both have kids now. I don't think most girls want to get married that young. Like my sister Mai. She wears cool clothes and makeup, and hangs out with her friends all the time. She's sixteen, but I can't imagine her married with kids.

A few weeks ago, I asked Mai if she would get married if Dad told her to.

"Are you kidding?" she answered. "I would rather die than get married when I'm still in high school. That's just a stupid Hmong custom."

"But what if Dad makes you?" I asked her.

She shrugged her shoulders and combed her beautiful dark hair that goes down to her butt. "He can't make me. I won't do it."

It kind of scared me when she said that. I always try to listen to my mom and dad. If you're Hmong, it's really important to respect your parents. We're different than the kids I see on TV or in the movies. They always talk back to their parents. I would never do that.

A few hours ago, I heard my sister screaming in the living room. My dad was yelling at her.

"You can't make me!" Mai shouted at him. "I'll kill myself before I get married to some stupid relative of ours!"

Then I heard my father say in Hmong, "It's our custom. You must respect our traditions."

"It's a stupid custom and a stupid culture!" she yelled at him. "You're in America now. Stop acting so old-fashioned!"

For a few seconds, the room was quiet. I don't think anyone has ever talked to my parents like that. They didn't know what to do. My father started to say something, but it was too late. Mai ran out of the house. On the way out she yelled, "I hate you both! If you really loved me, you wouldn't make me do this."

Then she was gone. It's freezing outside, and Mai wasn't wearing a jacket. I wonder where she went. Probably to a friend's house.

My parents didn't go after her. I wanted them to chase her down the street and tell her that it was okay. I wanted them to tell her that they wouldn't make her get married. Instead, they sat on the falling-apart sofa with kung fu pictures torn out of magazines taped to the wall above them, and didn't say anything for a long time. I could hear my mother crying and my father breathing really hard. WWF was on TV in my brothers' room. I sat on my bed next to the door and didn't move, waiting for something to happen.

Finally my father spoke. My parents always talk in Hmong with each other. "America is a bad place for us. There are many bad people. It makes our children disrespectful. People treat us like we are nothing and nobody understands our culture. Even our children don't care."

My mother was quiet for a minute and then she said, "I understand how important it is to follow the Hmong traditions, but maybe we need to think about this. Mai is still in high school. Why can't we wait until after she graduates? It's just a few more years."

Then I heard my father slap her hard on the cheek. She gasped.

"Why do you talk like this?" he yelled. "I know what's best. There's no reason to change our traditions now."

My mother's voice was very strong when she spoke next. She said, "You may not hit me, Blia. I am not your child, and I will not be disciplined by you. I will say what I think and you cannot stop me."

I was so proud of my mom. I hate it when Dad hits her. Our family is very traditional compared to many Hmong families here in America. These days, I don't think most Hmong men are so strict or feel so strongly about holding onto their traditions.

My dad fought for the Americans and was nearly killed many times. He came to America thinking people would treat him like a hero, but instead most treated him like garbage on the street. That's one of the reasons he's so angry at this country and why he really wants to hold onto the Hmong traditions.

There was a long silence and I could tell my father was shocked that she had talked back to him. Then he said quietly, "You're becoming one of them," but at least he didn't raise his voice.

There were so many feelings swirling around in my head, but I hoped maybe they would calm down if I concentrated on my homework for a while. When I came out of the room to get my backpack, my father saw me and said, "Choua, you're a good girl. I hope you don't do this to me when it's your turn to get married."

"I won't, Dad," I answered.

Now I am sitting at my desk thinking when will it be *my* turn? Could I be married in just a few years? I can't imagine getting married when I'm still in high school, and I hate the idea of my dad picking a man for me. What if my dad makes me marry an older traditional man from the clan who feels like he can hit me whenever he wants to? No thank you! There are a lot of Hmong girls who go to Como High

School who are already married. Most of them don't tell their teachers or non-Hmong kids. They just act like everything is the same. Then one day somebody notices that they're pregnant, and then everything changes for them.

I feel really sorry for Mai right now even though she dissed my parents. I'm 15 so I get crushes on boys all the time. Right now I really like this cute guy called Ku who's in my social studies class. I'll tell you more about him later.

When my little sister Nou was getting ready for bed, she asked, "Where's Mai?"

"She ran away from home," I answered.

"Why would she do that? Doesn't she like it here?" she asked me.

"You're too young to understand," I answered. "Besides, I don't want to talk about it."

Nou crawled into her bed next to mine. She was wearing dirty pajamas, and she hadn't washed up. My parents are so busy that sometimes the young ones don't get taken care of unless us older ones do it. They do what they can, but they use up all their energy trying to put food on the table and pay the rent. I think they're really stressed from their long hours at work. Sometimes my dad works overtime so he can make extra money, and then we don't see him for a long time.

I always make sure I'm clean. Sometimes I wash my own clothes in the sink instead of waiting to go to the laundromat. I began doing that a few years ago when some rich white kids started making fun of me. They said I always came to school dirty and that I had greasy hair. Then I got lice a few months later and my mom made me cut off all my hair. I missed three days of school because the school nurse told me I couldn't come back until they were all gone.

Tomorrow morning I'll make sure Nou has a bath and I'll look for some clean clothes for her. I wish I didn't have so much responsibility, but that's just the way it is.

Friday, November 3

I know I shouldn't say this, but I really don't like black kids. They talk back to the teachers, and they beat up other kids. I'm glad I'm in high school now so I don't have to go outside and play at recess. That sucked. A lot of black kids used to pick on my friends and me on the playground. I know not all black kids are like that, but I still don't like them.

At lunchtime, my friends and I hang out in the hallway now and talk about boys and stuff. The other day, my friend, Bee, stole some cigarettes from her brother. We hid in a bathroom stall during break and tried smoking them. I wanted to spit because my mouth felt like it was filled with hot dirty sand. I know some kids think it's cool to smoke, but I didn't like it at all. It made me gag.

Anyway, this is what happened at school today. I was at my locker getting my books together between first and second period when this black girl from my math class walked by and just knocked the books right out of my hands. I swear it wasn't an accident, and it really pissed me off. She's always trying to act tough and mouthing off at the teacher, but I've never had any trouble from her.

When I got to math class she was hanging out with some of her friends by the door.

"Hey, whassup, little Hmong girl?" she asked. I felt furious, but I was too scared to do anything. She looks like a WWF wrestler except she's got huge boobs. I bet she started wearing a bra in third grade. She's always walking around, sticking her chest in everyone's face, and trying to act like a know-it-all. Then she's always talking, trying to be the one who answers all the questions even though she's almost always wrong.

I'm the opposite. I hardly ever talk in class unless a teacher calls on me. Then I usually shrug my shoulders and say I don't know, even if I do. I wasn't always like that, but in sixth grade, Mr. Jackson asked me to read out loud during science class. I never minded reading out loud in ESL class where all the other kids were learning English, too, but it made me nervous to do it in front of all the good readers in regular class. I'm a pretty good reader, but sometimes I make mistakes. So anyway, I was feeling really nervous and when I got to the word *muscle*, I pronounced it *mus-kul* instead of *mus-sel*, the way it's supposed to be. The whole class laughed at me. I ignored them and kept on reading. Then I screwed up some more, and read *is-land* instead of *iland*. I know how to say that damn word, but I was so embarrassed that I wasn't thinking straight. That was the day I decided I wouldn't open my mouth in class anymore. I figure it's better not to be noticed than to say something that humiliates me.

The only place I don't feel like that is in Ms. Martinez's class. I like to talk in there and even read my stories to the class. That's because she's really kind and a good listener, and it's also because the only rule she has in her class is "no put downs." Nobody ever even tries in her class. They all respect her too much. Nobody wants to disappoint her.

So back to my story. There was this big black girl blocking the doorway and I didn't know what to do.

"Could you please move, Leticia?" I said quietly.

"Oh, so the little Hmong girl can talk!" she said.

I wanted to spit on her, but I took a deep breath and said, "Listen, I don't want any trouble. Just let me in."

"Did you hear that?" she said. "She doesn't want any trouble. If you don't be wanting any trouble, then stay the hell out of my way, little girl."

I don't think I've ever been so angry in my whole life. I pushed past Leticia and her friends and went to my desk. Mr. Cho walked in and class started a few seconds later so nothing else happened. All through class I had to keep taking deep gulps of air to keep my whole body from shaking.

There's this other black girl in my class who sits behind me. She talks differently from the other kids, and she's a little bit hard to understand. I always thought she seemed nice, even though we'd never talked before. After class she came up to me and said, "You should just ignore Leticia. She's a bitch."

I was surprised that she talked to me. Usually only other Hmong kids talk to me.

"Thanks," I said and I smiled at her.

"That's okay," she said. "You seem really nice, but you should stick up for yourself more."

"What do you mean?" I asked.

"You Hmong kids are always so quiet. Some people think you're not very smart because you never talk, but I don't. I like Hmong kids."

"Oh yeah?" I said. It was time for me to meet my friends, Bee and Trisha, at my locker for lunch, and I was anxious to get going.

"Yeah," she said. "Are you in ESL?"

"Not anymore," I answered. I was surprised she knew what ESL was.

"I used to be in ESL classes when I was in elementary school and there were lots of Hmong kids in my class. At first they were mean to me. Some of the boys said I was ugly and loud. They laughed at the way I talked too, but then they got to know me. After a while, we became friends."

"You were in ESL?" I asked. "How come?" I couldn't figure out why a black kid would need to go to ESL class.

"Because I'm from Liberia," she said. "We talk English there, but it's kind of different from American English. Actually, I don't really fit in anywhere. The African American kids think I'm a freak because I don't talk and act like them, and all the other kids think I'm just another African American. It's kind of lonely."

Before I talked to her, I thought all the black kids were African

American except for the Somali kids who go to ESL. Usually I just think Asian kids need help with their English. One of my good friends, Trisha, is Vietnamese. She still goes to ESL for help in science and math.

I didn't really know what to say after that, but she didn't seem to care. "My name is Frankie," she said. "Don't worry, I won't let Leticia give you any trouble."

I was going to tell her to forget it, but I decided to see if she really would.

"Thanks, Frankie," I said. "That's really nice."

Monday, November 6

It's been four days since Mai ran away. At first I wasn't so worried because she has good friends I know will take care of her, but yesterday I started to freak out. Why didn't she call to say she was all right?

Then the phone rang and my mom picked it up. She listened for a minute and then said in her funny English, "Wait, please. I get my girl."

My mom has a hard time talking on the phone or getting help at the store. She finally started taking lessons last year. She usually gets Mai or me to help her.

"*Cua los pab kuv*," she yelled out in Hmong which means "Choua, come here and help me."

I picked up the phone and a lady said very loudly and slowly, "Do you speak English?"

It makes me crazy when people talk like that, like they think we're deaf or something.

"Yes, I understand English," I answered.

She continued in that stupid, loud voice. "I'm phoning from the Wausau Police Department in Wisconsin. I want to tell you that we have a girl name Mai Vang in our custody. Is she your sister?"

My stomach did a somersault. "Yes," I answered. Then I whispered to my mom in Hmong, "They found Mai. She's in Wausau."

We have cousins in Wausau. It's about three hours from the Cities. I wondered what she was doing there.

"Listen carefully," the woman said. "Your sister is being moved to the juvenile detention center. That's like a jail for teenagers. She's going to stay until her court date in two weeks."

"What?" I said. "Can't we come get her and take her home?"

"No, you can't," she answered. "Your sister was caught in a stolen car with two Hmong boys. They said they were on their way to California."

My mom was tugging on my sleeve, whispering for me to tell her what was going on. I felt like I might faint. Mai with two boys in a stolen car? She would never do that. And California? Why would she go there?

"Are you still there?" the lady asked.

"Yes," I answered, "but my sister would never do that. I don't think it's her."

"Are your parents Mai Houa Xiong and Blia Vang?"

"Yes."

"Do you live on Sherburne Avenue in Saint Paul?"

"Yes."

"Then this is your sister."

I didn't know what to say. There was a short silence, and then she told me to get a pen so she could give me directions to the detention center. She said we could come visit as soon as we were able to drive there, but she repeated that we couldn't take Mai home.

After I hung up, I told my mother everything. She started crying and the other kids (all except my older brother, Ger, who is never home) came into the kitchen to find out what was going on. My father wasn't there because he was working a late shift at the electronics factory where he assembles microchips for computers.

My mother said everyone needed to get ready for bed. She told me to stay up so I could tell my dad everything the lady had told me. So here I am sitting on my bed. I feel just sick about what's going on with my sister. I really don't want to tell my dad about it. He's going to kill her.

I wish I could just close my eyes and make this all disappear. Why is everything so messed up?

Tuesday, November 7

My dad didn't get home until really late last night. When I told him what happened to Mai, he said, "I don't care if she's dead or not. She's not my daughter." My dad is very strong and doesn't show feelings like sadness or love very often. Mostly he just shows anger. I know that he didn't mean what he said.

I didn't know what to do. I sat beside him on the sofa with my head down and my hands in my lap. I wanted to hug him like kids do on TV, but I didn't think he would like that.

I stared at the picture of General Vang Pao on the wall. He's a famous Hmong military leader and most Hmong families have a picture of him in their houses. Maybe it's kind of like having a picture of Jesus if you're a Christian, but I'm not sure.

After a long time, my dad got up and said in Hmong, "Go to bed, Choua. You're a good girl, not like your sister. Never do this to us, Choua. Your mother and I are full of shame. Mai has betrayed our family."

It felt like all of my fear and sadness were rolled up in a big snowball that kept getting bigger and bigger. I got up and went to my room, but I had a hard time falling asleep.

My mother woke me up early this morning to tell me my married sister, Youa, was sick. She usually comes to baby-sit my brothers and sister Pao, Jerry and Ia during the day. They're not in school yet. Mom said I had to stay home today and take care of them. Mai and I usually take turns baby-sitting when Youa can't come. In sixth grade, I stayed home a lot to help out because Youa was pregnant with Bao and she felt sick and was always puking. Whenever my teacher, Mr. Olsen, asked me why I wasn't at school, I told him I was sick, but I knew he didn't believe me.

At conference time, he told my parents that they were in America now and parents couldn't keep their children home to baby-sit. I knew my parents were very angry, but they just nodded and said they understood. The problem is that most teachers *don't* understand. My parents don't have any extra money to pay a sitter and we can't just leave the babies alone! It's the older brother or sister's duty to stay home and take care of the kids. There's no other choice. Sometimes I just wish teachers would get off our backs. Don't they realize we're not white kids? In our culture, family is everything. We have to take care of each other.

So I stayed home today. I tried to help my mom by cleaning the kitchen. I put everything away, washed and dried the dishes, and scrubbed the table and the counters. I also gave the kids a bath, and put them in clean clothes, but they kept pooping and crying and throwing food. After lunch, I wondered why I had even tried since they were all dirty again and so was the kitchen. It's hard work taking care of kids—a lot harder than school.

I have a ton of homework to do. I should be doing it right now, but I feel better when I write. Who cares if I don't get my homework finished? Who cares if I get bad grades? I'll never have a chance to go to college anyway. We don't have the money and I'm not smart enough to get a scholarship. I'll probably just end up getting a job at Target or something.

Ms. Martinez always tells her students we can be anything we want. She says I can be a great writer, and she always talks to me about going to college. I try to look interested when she's talking, but

I know it probably won't happen, especially if my dad makes me get married. (I'm sorry if you're reading this, Ms. Martinez I don't want to hurt your feelings, but I have to think about real life, not a fairy tale.)

I really want to believe that I can be anything I want, but right now I just don't. I worked really hard today, mostly so I wouldn't have to think about Mai in that prison. I wanted to ask my parents this morning when they were going to see her and if I could come along, but I was too scared. So I don't know what's going on. I still can't believe she stole a car and ran away.

You know what? I think I'll go and talk to my mom right now. I need to know what's going on. I'll tell you what happens when I come back.

A Few Minutes Later

I'm back. My mom was in the kitchen washing up so I started to help her out. I was quiet for a few minutes and then I asked her, "Did you go see Mai today?"

She nodded her head, but didn't say anything.

"How is she?"

"I think she very sad and very angry," she answered in English. These days she's trying to talk in English more instead of always talking Hmong. "She not want to see your father. She hurt him very bad, Choua. I not understand why she do this." She started crying again.

"Did she tell you about the stolen car and the boys?" I asked her.

"No, she say nothing. She not want to talk about it." Then she put down her dish towel and put her hands on my shoulders. She looked very serious. "Choua," she said, "you talk to her. She love you. She tell you why. Please, you go Friday with sister, Youa. She drive you. But not tell father."

My mother was whispering. My father was on the phone in the other room. "You not go to school Friday, okay? Ka take care of babies. If get home late, you tell father you stay after school with teacher. Okay?"

"Okay, Mom," I said, and I went back to my room.

So I get to see Mai in a few days. I'm excited, but scared, too. Mostly, I'm just sad.

Friday, November 10

Yesterday I couldn't concentrate at school. I didn't even think about big black Leticia and her stupid friends. I finally told Trisha and Bee that Mai had run away. I'm not sure why I didn't say anything until now. Maybe I'm kind of embarrassed. The more I write in this journal, the more worried I get about sharing it with other kids. It's really private. I don't know if other people should know all about my family's secrets. What if kids at school guess it's me?

Ms. M. says to just keep writing and to not worry. She says I can take out the really private parts later on if I feel uncomfortable. I just feel so much better when I write down all the bad stuff that's happening to me, like throwing up after eating some nasty food. So I guess I'll just carry on.

Frankie was waiting for me at my locker before Math yesterday. When she saw me she said, "Girl, where were you? I waited for you like I said I would and you never showed."

It made me feel really good that she would do that for me. Whenever I felt sad, I thought about how sweet that was, and it helped me feel better. I know it's not a big deal, but it's nice to know that someone is thinking of me.

But I want to write about seeing Mai today. My sister Youa and I left for Wausau at about 7:00 in the morning. She brought her two kids, Bao and Cindy. It was a long drive, and we had a hard time finding the juvenile detention center once we got into town. It was way out of town, tucked away in a little forest. The kids were crying and puking in the back seat almost the whole way there. We had to stop a bunch of times to clean them up and change their diapers. When we finally got there it was almost lunchtime.

Mai in Jail

It was a depressing place. There were a bunch of kids there, maybe 20. I noticed some Hmong guys and I tried to guess which ones stole the car with Mai. The rest were white kids except for one black boy. They were all wearing the same thing: blue pants and sweatshirts. It reminded me of patients on TV hospital shows.

We waited at a table in the corner. Mai didn't look very excited to see us. She actually looked kind of angry.

"I can only talk for ten minutes," she said. "I have to eat in a few minutes."

"Can't you eat later?" I asked. "It took us a long time to get here."

"Does this look like a hotel?" she answered. "In case you haven't noticed, I'm in a jail here."

Youa and I looked at each other. We didn't know what to say. I wanted to reach out and give Mai a hug, but she looked like she might bite me. Youa's kids were crumpling up paper on the table and making a lot of noise, but we ignored them. After a while, a nice man named Marshall came over and brought them some crayons. I think he was a guard, but he was wearing jeans and a regular shirt, not a uniform.

"Where are Mom and Dad?" Mai asked, looking around like she expected them to be hiding in a corner.

"They're not coming today. Mom sent me and I'm not supposed to tell Dad I came," I told her.

"I hope I never see him again," she said. "What a bastard!"

God, she was mean!

Youa ignored her and said, "Tell us what happened, Mai. We were so worried about you."

"There's nothing to tell," she answered. "I went to see my home-boys after I ran away. I knew they would take care of me."

I noticed she had hickeys, like someone had been sucking on her neck really hard. It made me feel worried so I looked away.

"Who are they?" Youa asked.

"Just friends," Mai shrugged. "Guys I know from school."

"So what happened?" Youa asked. I could tell she was trying to act like a parent, but she's still so young, too. She's just a few years older than Mai.

"I hid out in Fong's room for the night, and we went to school the next day. After school we met up with Johnny and decided it was time to get the hell out of Saint Paul."

"How did you steal the car?" I asked. I was kind of curious.

"It was easy," she said. "We just broke into Fong's uncle's house, took his keys, and then took the car. No big deal."

It seemed like a big deal to me, but I didn't say so.

"What about the boys?" I asked. "Why did they want to run away?"

"They hate their families, too. And life is so boring. You can't do anything in a Hmong family. Everyone wants to get away from their parents, Choua," Mai answered.

"I don't get it," I said. I didn't really feel that way.

"They always try to control you. They tell you what to do all the time, and we're never allowed to go anywhere or do anything."

It's true. Hmong girls aren't supposed to go out except to school. You're supposed to come home right after school and do your home-work and help out. I hate that. My dad often works at night so then it's easier because Mom doesn't mind as much. She just doesn't want us to get into trouble.

Then Mai blurted out some more. "Then they just want you to get out of the house and marry some older man from the clan. It's a stupid culture. I hate it. I don't want to be Hmong anymore."

"But you *are*," I whispered. Being Hmong is the biggest part of me. How can you run away from that?

"But I don't have to act like I am," Mai answered. "When I'm with my friends and my homeboys, I can do anything that I want. I can party and drink and smoke, and no one can tell me what to do."

I really didn't know Mai was doing all kinds of bad stuff. If my parents knew, they would have a heart attack.

Mai was allowed to bring her tray to the table and eat with us while all the other kids sat together and laughed and talked. She kept looking over at them like she would rather be with them than us. The food looked disgusting, even worse than school lunch, and I was glad we had stopped at McDonald's on the way.

Mai told us about how they stole some money from Fong and Johnny's parents, and then how they went to Fong's grandmother and took some money from her, too. She told me right to my face that she had done all this awful stuff, and she didn't even seem ashamed.

Youa looked very serious, and I could tell she had something on her mind. "Mai, are you in a gang?" she asked.

Mai started to laugh and threw back her long hair over her shoulder. Mai is very beautiful, but at that moment she looked like the evil queen from *Snow White*.

"You really don't know anything, do you?" she said.

"What do you mean?" Youa asked.

"First off, there's nothing wrong with being in a gang. They protect you. They're your homeboys. If something goes wrong, they take care of you. My gang is like my family."

What? I couldn't believe my sister was in a gang!

"How long?" Youa asked

"I don't know. Maybe a year. It's a good thing I am or Dad would probably have me married to some pervert by now. At least I had someone to run to."

I hadn't talked in a long time. I felt like I was sitting in a theater and watching an exciting movie. The only thing missing was the popcorn. I know in gangs there are lots of guns. Usually the girls or the young boys have to carry the guns so they're the ones who take the fall if the police catch them. I know there's lots of drinking and drugs, and that they steal from mostly Hmong people because they know people from their own community probably won't go to the police. I know that boys get beat up when they join a gang, and that girls are sometimes raped by all the guys in the gang when they join. That's the thing that worried me most of all.

"What did you have to do to get in the gang?" I asked her.

"Oh, stop being such an innocent little girl, Choua," Mai hissed at me. "Just grow up! If you're asking me if I've ever screwed around with my homeboys, the answer is yes. If you're asking me if I've ever smoked pot, the answer is yes. What else do you want to know?"

I tried not to look at the hickeys on her neck. I tried not to imagine her doing those things or having those things done to her, but it didn't work.

"Nothing," I answered. I didn't want to hear anything else. I wanted to get away from her. I felt like I didn't know her, and I knew I didn't like her.

"I can't believe you're both so innocent," she said. "What about Ger? He's been in a gang for years! Why do you think he's never at home? The only difference between him and me is that Dad doesn't care what he does because he's a boy! Boys can do whatever they like and it doesn't matter."

~~~

It was a long drive home so there was lots of time to talk. The babies were asleep, and Youa was playing some Korean pop music. It was raining and the car was nice and warm. I felt sleepy.

Youa and I are not very close because she is about five years older than me, and it seems like a long time ago when she lived at home. I really like her, but we have never really talked about anything important before.

Youa lives with her husband, Tou, at his parents' house. He's a mechanic at a Hmong garage. I feel kind of sorry for her. She works all day at our house, and then she comes home and cooks dinner for Tou's mom and dad and his brothers and sisters. Plus, she needs to take care of her own kids. I think her life must suck. It's way too much work. I don't want to have to work that hard when I'm married, and I hope I don't have to live with my husband's parents. Youa and Tou never get any privacy, and her in-laws are always on her back to do this and do that. I would hate that.

We were quiet for a while and then Youa said, "Choua, I hope you don't turn out like Mai. I'm worried that you'll get into a gang, too."

"Are you crazy?" I asked.

I would *never* get into a gang. I have my family and friends. I don't need a gang.

"Did you know Ger was in a gang, too?" she asked.

"No, of course not. I don't know anything," I answered. I was just as surprised as she was to hear the news about Ger. I noticed he was never home, but I thought maybe he had a girlfriend or was just out with his friends. I wonder what kind of bad things he is doing. I wonder if he ever steals or if he has sex or does drugs. I just can't believe he would do any of those things.

Ger's in twelfth grade at Harding High School. He transferred there from Como when he got his driver's license in tenth grade. A lot of his friends went there and he wanted to hang with them. He's super popular, and the girls really like him. They're always phoning the house, giggling and then hanging up. Ger is also *very* smart and he's kind, too. When I was having a hard time with math in elementary school, he used to drill me every night on my times tables. I've always thought of him as the perfect Hmong guy, the kind I'd like to date.

"What do you know about gangs, Choua?" Youa asked me. "Has anyone ever talked to you about them?"

She was trying to be like a mother again. I know she really loves us kids, and she thinks we don't get enough attention, but it felt weird.

"Listen, Youa," I said, "I know all about gangs. Believe me, I'm not going to get into one. But what about Mai and Ger? Do you think we should tell Mom and Dad?"

"If they don't know about Mai yet, I think they're going to find out soon. They have a meeting with a Hmong social worker on Monday. But I don't know about Ger. Maybe Tou can talk to him. He used to be in a gang, you know."

"Tou? You're kidding, right?" Tou seems like such a nice guy. He's not the type.

"No, I'm not kidding," she said, turning down the Korean music. "He joined the Asian Crips in tenth grade. He joined because he wanted to be popular. When he started dating me and wanted to get out, it was almost impossible. They wouldn't let him leave. You know how it is. They were scared he'd get into another gang and rat them out. He didn't get out until he married me."

Tou hardly ever comes to our house, and my parents act like he isn't even there when he comes to visit. I wondered if it was because of the gang thing.

"I wasn't allowed to go on dates, but I was like Mai," Youa continued. "I wanted to be like the American girls—you know—meet someone and fall in love."

"So? Did you fall in love with Tou?" I asked her.

"Yeah. I met him when we were in tenth grade. He was so fine. All the girls had crushes on him. I didn't think he would ever notice me."

"So what happened?" I asked her.

"Well, some friends and I started following him around and he finally noticed me. We were the most popular Hmong couple at school. We were always together, hanging out at our lockers, necking and skipping classes."

Youa just doesn't seem like the wild type to me. It almost made me laugh to think about her and Tou kissing at their lockers and skipping out. They're so married now.

"You're kidding? Didn't you get in trouble?" I asked.

"Yeah, a bit, but never enough for Mom and Dad to find out."

"Did you know he was in a gang?" I asked.

"Not at first. I was too in love to notice. By the time I found out, I was pregnant."

"What?" I gasped. "Oh my God, you were pregnant before you got married?" I just sat there, stunned. I turned up the Korean music again because I didn't know what to say.

You know what I feel like? Like I've been sitting outside on a pitch dark night. Then the sun comes out of nowhere and almost blinds me, and I find myself sitting beside these people who sounded like my family when they were talking in the dark, but when I actually see them, they're total strangers. Maybe this is what growing up is all about. I'm not sure I like it.

After a bit, Youa told me some more. "After Tou found out I was pregnant, he got real serious. He said he wanted to support the baby, and he'd do whatever he had to. He wanted to be a man about it. We had to go tell Mom and Dad. I'll never forget it."

"What happened?" I asked. I imagined flames shooting out of my father's eyes and starting Youa on fire.

"Well, Tou's father and two of his brothers came along with us. They told Dad what happened and that Tou had to marry me. At first Dad said he would never let me marry a man who got me pregnant."

"But you *did* marry him," I said. "Why did he change his mind?"

"Tou's father reminded Dad that I was no good anymore. No man would ever want me because I was used. Then Dad finally agreed. He told me to get out of the house. Tou's parents had to pay a bride price, but it was a lot less than usual. That's because I was a bad woman."

She paused and took a deep breath. "I made a terrible mistake, Choua, and I paid for it."

I swear, I will never do something crazy like getting pregnant no matter how much I love a guy.

"How long after that did you get married?" I asked her.

"The next week at Tou's house. There was no party like there usually is. It was a terrible day. I got dressed up in my traditional clothes, and Mom and Dad came, but they left right after the ceremony. None of you kids even came. I cried and cried. I didn't want to be pregnant and I didn't want to be married. I just wanted to be a normal teenage girl going around with a cute guy. It took a long time for Mom to forgive me. I don't know if Dad has. He still hates Tou."

The kids were starting to fuss in the back seat. Suddenly I felt sorry for Youa.

I remember coming over to her house when I was younger and playing with Tou's brothers and sisters. I have never wondered if Youa is happy or what her life is like. I honestly don't think I wonder about anyone. I'm too busy thinking about myself. I wonder if that's normal for a teenager or if I'm just a selfish bitch.

"Well, what happened then?" I asked.

"Well, I didn't quit school," she said. "I kept going until I was almost ready to have Bao. But I felt like a freak. I went from being the cool Hmong girl to being the pregnant Hmong girl with no friends."

"What about Tou?"

"He had to quit school to make money for the baby," she answered. "So I was alone. All the kids in the gang started to ignore me, and my other friends didn't understand. I was so lonely."

"Why didn't you quit?"

"I wanted to quit school more than anything else. But I knew I couldn't," Youa told me.

"Why not?"

"Because this is America, Choua," she answered. "If you quit school, there are no chances for a better life."

"But Mom never even went to school and none of the Aunties did either," I said.

"Maybe that was okay in Laos. Most of the people were farmers there. Here you need to work hard to make enough money to survive. And here women can do more. We can be somebody. If I want my daughters to finish school and go to college, then I have to do it, too. I need to be an example. I never want them to do what I did. As soon as the kids are in school, I'm going to college."

I don't know any Hmong women who have gone to college. I think it's really tight that Youa is going to. I wish more Hmong women were like that. (Remember I said the other day that I couldn't, go to college? I *really, really* want to if I can. And I don't think I ever want to have babies. It would be too hard.)

"Choua, in this country, education is one of the most important things," Youa said. "Don't forget it. You're so smart. That's why I hate to think about you getting mixed up with some bad kids or in a gang."

"You can stop worrying," I said. "I'm not like that."

"Promise me you won't get in a gang," Youa said.

"Okay, okay. I promise!"

Monday, November 13

Sometimes you do something that nobody ever thought you would do, and you are the most surprised of all. That's what happened today on this purple, gray day that seemed like it was going to be perfectly ordinary when I woke up this morning.

Trisha was waiting for me by my locker when I got to school. I don't think I've told you about her. She's Vietnamese. She has a long, thin body like a pencil, and the longest eyelashes I have ever seen. Even her smile is long—it stretches across her face like a rubber band when she smiles. Her hair is long too and always perfectly parted down the middle.

"Follow me," she said. I noticed she was wearing blue eye shadow and lip gloss.

"I can't. First bell is going to ring in a minute," I answered, fiddling with my combination lock. I always forget the numbers when I'm in a hurry.

"Do you *always* have to follow the rules, Choua?" she asked. She had an edge in her voice, like a sharp knife.

"Oh, maybe she's right," I thought as I finally swung the metal door open to show off my magazine pictures of pretty Asian singers and models. I don't know why I keep them up there—maybe so I can pretend I'm looking in a mirror and I really look like that. I wish!

"Okay, okay," I said. "Where are we going?"

"Just follow me," she said, closing my locker for me. "And you won't need your books."

We walked to the student parking lot, and I kept turning around to see if any teachers would chase us down. The parking lot was full of cars and buses, but no people.

"There he is," she said, pointing to a cute boy, standing beside a red Chevy Malibu. He was wearing a Minnesota Vikings jacket, with his hands jammed in the pockets. He was tall, like Trisha, his hair was greased back, and he was white.

"Trisha, what are we doing and who is *he*?" I asked. He looked kind of familiar.

"Don't you recognize him? That's Ken Olsen! He's only the star basketball player at Como."

"Oh my God, you're right," I said. "We're meeting *him*?"

"Yes, we are," she said. "I met him in the parking lot after school. He thinks I'm a senior and I just moved here from California so don't you dare blow my cover!"

"He thinks you're a senior?" I whispered in shock. "He's going to find out, Trisha! Then what?"

"Shut up!" she said, as she took her lip gloss out of her pocket and smoothed some more across her lips. "How do I look?"

"Like you're a sophomore!" I answered.

She ignored me and marched over to Ken. "Hi Ken," she said. "This is my friend, Choua. Is it okay if she joins us?"

"Hi, Choua," he said. "Are you new here, too?" Most of the older kids don't hang with the tenth graders. They never notice us.

"Yeah," I lied. "I just got here last week." Close up, Ken was even more handsome than he was from far away.

"Let's drive over to Como Park and smoke some pot," he said.

I felt really scared. I wanted to rush back to the music class I was missing and forget this ever happened, but someone had to stay and protect Trisha. What if he tried to attack her?

"Sure," said Trisha, acting like she was the coolest thing on the planet. "That's tight." Then she looked at me, and widened her eyes, like she was trying to say, "Come on, stupid!" I noticed how long her eyelashes were again and how pretty she was.

I didn't know what else to do. I got into the back seat of the car that was covered with black fur. There were fuzzy red dice dangling from the rearview mirror, and Christina A. was blaring out of the radio. We drove across Lexington Parkway and parked the car in a big parking lot next to a forested part of the park. We walked over to a group of trees that were far away from the road and huddled underneath them. I was shaking a bit. It's getting cold, but I'm still wearing my powder blue spring jacket because it's styling, and also because I don't have a winter jacket. I hope my Mom lets me buy a new one this year. I don't want to wear ripped-up, stained hand-me-downs from Mai or Ger.

Ken took a joint and an orange Bic lighter out of his pocket. He lit the joint, took a deep puff, and held his breath. It smelled sweet, nicer than cigarette smoke.

"Here you go," he said, handing it to Trisha. I know she'd never smoked pot before. She took the joint and put it in her mouth, acting as if she knew exactly what she was doing. She took a deep puff and started coughing and choking. She couldn't stop.

Ken started laughing. "You've never done this before, huh? You'll catch on. Here, let me show you." He moved next to her, so their hips were touching on the soft, mossy ground. He showed her how to suck in the smoke and hold it in her mouth.

"How about you, Choua?" he asked, and I have to admit, my heart skipped a beat. I know he liked Trisha, not me, but it was a thrill just to have a cute boy like that remember my name!

I blushed and shook my head. "No thanks, not today."

"Oh come on," he said, smiling at me. I noticed two dimples on his cheeks covered with blond peach fuzz. "I won't tell anyone. Just this one time. You should try it to see what it's like."

They were both looking at me. Did everyone think I was such a little Miss Perfect? Suddenly I felt like a loser because I had never smoked pot before, like I was the only kid on the planet who had never done it. So I took the joint from Ken, put it in my mouth, and he bent over and lit it for me. He was so close to me that I could smell his sweaty, warm body. My breath quickened and I took a deep puff. The smoke felt hot and sweet in my lungs and it hurt like hell. I coughed, but not as bad as Trisha.

At first I didn't feel anything, but in a minute or so, the world seemed suddenly lighter and funnier, like splashing in a pool on a hot summer day. I started to laugh and couldn't stop. Trisha was laughing too.

Ken said, "I've got to go take a pee," and we laughed even harder.

"See this is fun, isn't it?" she said after he left. "Aren't you glad you came?"

At that moment, I *did* feel kind of glad. I was having fun.

"Listen, Choua, I panicked when I met him yesterday by the buses. I had to tell him I was a senior or I didn't think he'd talk to me. Don't say anything, *pleaaaase*?"

Ken came back and sat down right next to Trisha. He reached over and touched her hair. "You're really pretty, you know," he said.

"Why don't you come a little closer?"

It felt like I was reading a romance book, only the pictures were right there in front of me, instead of in my mind. He started to softly kiss her, and I saw her mouth open just a little bit. Was that a tongue? His hand was on her neck and then her back. I was sure it would be moving under her clothes any minute.

I couldn't watch any longer. I didn't want to leave Trisha alone with him because he was getting pretty excited and who knew what could happen next, but I also didn't want to watch them kiss anymore, either. I got up off the cold ground.

"I've got to go," I said.

"No, don't go," Trisha said. "Just stay a few more minutes."

"She can go if she wants," Ken said. "See you later, Choua." He suddenly seemed anxious to get rid of me. I'm sure he was ready to put his hand under her sweater, and he didn't want me staring.

"Choua, *please* stay," Trisha said. I could tell she wanted to keep kissing him, but she was scared of being alone with him.

"Trisha, you should come too. We've got the tenth grade assembly in half an hour. It's going to take us almost that long to walk back."

As soon as I said it, I knew I had messed up.

"You're a sophomore?" Ken said, straightening up. "You told me you were a senior!"

Trisha didn't know what to say. She looked really embarrassed. She pushed herself off the ground and dusted off her butt. "Come on, Choua, let's get out of here." She grabbed me by the arm and we ran across Lexington Parkway, toward the school.

"Thanks a lot!" she said, after we stopped running to catch our breaths. "How could you do that to me?"

"I'm really sorry," I said. "It just came out." I was quiet for a few seconds. "You know he was going to find out sooner or later."

She ignored me. "You've ruined everything," she said, and then she turned around and started walking in the opposite direction of the school. I walked back alone, staring at the green water of the lake and the gray sky. I shivered. I felt terrible: terrible that Trisha was mad at me, and terrible that I had been stupid enough to smoke pot. Life is getting worse and worse. I'm going to call Trisha in a few minutes to see if she's forgiven me.

Tuesday, November 14

Sometimes things surprise you in a good way. Like today. Yesterday felt like a rotting banana, all soft and spotty. I felt guilty and worried about everything that happened. I called Trisha and we talked for a bit, but I could tell she was still mad even though she said she wasn't.

"Just forget it," she said. "We can talk tomorrow."

Today feels more like big, crunchy red apple that explodes with sweet bubbles in your mouth when you bite into it. It started out the same as always: me waiting for Trisha by my locker. She didn't show, and I was worried that she skipped out again. While I was waiting, Frankie came along, wearing big hoop earrings, her hair all bushy and wild looking. My hair is all limp and greasy unless I wash it every day. I wanted to touch hers to see what it felt like.

"Hey Choua," she said. "Let's go! It's time for math. Remember? I'm going to protect you!"

Frankie is really sweet, even if she is kind of weird. As soon as I saw her today, I knew I would let her be my friend. Bee and Trisha are great, but we need some new people in our group. We've hung out since eighth grade at Ramsey Junior, and we haven't really made any new friends, except people we say "hi" to.

"Can you wait just a sec?" I asked. "My friend is supposed to meet me here. We need to talk about something important."

"What do you need to talk about?" she asked.

I didn't think it was any of her business. I was going to say "It's kind of private," but then it all came tumbling out. I told her about skipping out with Trisha and smoking pot yesterday, and I told her about Mai in the juvenile detention center and even about how Ger is in a gang. I don't know why I did it. Once I got started, I couldn't stop. It surprised me because I'm usually very good about keeping secrets.

By that time, we were really late for math class so Frankie said, "Can I have lunch with you and your friends? Maybe we can talk some more then."

I didn't know how Bee and Trisha would feel about it. I'm sure they had never had lunch with a black girl before.

I thought for just a second and then said, "Sure, why not?" Things were so messed up already. I didn't see how this could make things any worse.

So at lunch Bee and Trisha met me at my locker and so did Frankie. I was so relieved when Trisha showed up. I was scared she might never hang with me again.

"Everyone," I said, "this is Frankie. She's in my math class. She's going to have lunch with us today."

They looked at me like I was crazy, but then they smiled shyly and said, "Hi, Frankie. It's nice to meet you."

We went down to the lunchroom and had hamburgers and fries and corn. "Oh, I shouldn't eat this. I'll get too fat," Frankie said.

We looked at her and laughed.

"You're not fat," Trisha said.

"Oh, yes I am," she said. "Look at my big butt!"

That made us laugh again. "I don't even have a butt," I said. It's true. My jeans hang straight down. Today I wore my bellbottoms, platforms, and a GIRL'S RULE tee shirt I stole from Mai's drawer this morning. I wish I could gain a little weight and grow a little. When I looked in the mirror this morning I thought I looked like a sixth grader.

Trisha and I didn't have a chance to talk at lunch, but we all had a good time anyway. Frankie told us a lot of things that made us laugh. She told us how her sister always makes out with her boyfriend in the car and whenever her mom gets into the car she says, "What's that funny smell?" She told us about the food she eats—something called *fufu* I think, and how she goes to a church where they all clap and dance and scream "Praise Jesus!" Her life seems so different from mine. Bee and Trisha were really surprised, just like I was, when Frankie told them she used to be an ESL student.

"Are there any other Liberian kids at this school?" Bee asked.

"Nope, I'm the only one."

"Then you can be part of our gang," Bee said, and she smiled at me and Trisha. We need four to make it an even number."

We're not a gang, of course, just good friends. I didn't like that Bee called us a gang, but she doesn't know about Mai and Ger so I guess it's okay. I thought it was really nice that she asked Frankie to join us. When Frankie smiled, she looked like the sun. It made me laugh with happiness.

Thursday, November 16

Today Trisha and I finally got a chance to talk. After supper I told my mom I was going to the Lexington Library to study.

"But it dark, Choua," my mother protested. "I not want you go out."

"I'll be careful, Mom, I promise," I said. "And I'll be home by nine thirty."

Before my mom had a chance to say anything else, I grabbed my backpack and jacket and ran out of the house. That probably made her angry, but I didn't care. I had to talk to Trisha and make things right with her. Besides, I'm so tired of being stuck at home all the time, and I didn't lie to my mom, exactly. We did meet at the library only we didn't stay there. Instead we walked down University Avenue towards Target. It was kind of cold and I didn't have a hat or gloves.

Trisha looked warm in a purple hat and gloves that matched her puffy new ski jacket. Sometimes I feel jealous of her great clothes. The only great stuff I wear is what I steal from Mai, but I can't do that every day or she'll catch me. These days, Ka and I wear her stuff all the time since she's still in the detention center.

"Listen Trisha," I said as we walked without talking, our breaths blowing out white clouds into the darkness. "I'm really sorry about what happened the other day. I really screwed things up."

"I know you're sorry," Trisha said. "It's okay." She shoved her hands in her pocket and walked a little faster. "Anyway, I think it's

probably best that you messed up. It was pretty stupid to meet Ken, and we never should have smoked that pot."

I started to laugh. "It was weird, wasn't it? How did it make you feel?"

"Kind of sleepy and silly at the same time. I felt like I was watching myself in a movie or something."

"I know what you mean. I kind of felt that way too." I laughed a little nervously. "I don't know if I want to smoke pot again."

"Good," she said. "I don't think I want to, either." She looked kind of relieved. "It was fun and all, but remember all that stuff we learned in DARE back in fifth grade? It just doesn't seem very smart to smoke."

"I agree," I said. I was so glad we were talking and she wasn't angry anymore.

We walked without talking until we got to Target.

"Want to go in?" I asked.

"Sure," she said, "Let's get warm before we go back. I promised my mom I'd be home by nine thirty."

"Me too," I said.

Trisha lives in an apartment with her mom on University Avenue. Her mom works at a Vietnamese restaurant as a cook. She's gone most evenings so Trisha is all alone. Her parents are divorced and she hardly ever sees her dad. He lives in Wisconsin somewhere. She has an older sister, but she has a job in California and only comes home for holidays. Trisha must get lonely. I think about my huge family and how sometimes I wish they would shut up and leave me alone. Then I feel jealous of Trisha and her life. She can do pretty much whatever she wants, and she gets a lot more clothes and CDs and cool stuff because her mom doesn't have to buy junk for any brothers and sisters like my parents do. But I still think I'd rather have all my annoying brothers and sisters around than be alone all the time.

Trisha had a little money so we shared a Coke in the cafeteria at Target.

"So what about Ken?" I asked. "What's going to happen when you run into him in the hallway?"

"I'll just have to ignore him, I guess," she answered. "I'm sure he's already found some other girl to feel up. I bet he'll do it with anyone. It's not like I was anything special."

Personally, I think she is something special. I don't think any boy would ever want to do that with *me*.

"By the way," she added, "I shouldn't have kissed him. That was stupid."

"Well, it was kind of scary," I said. "What if he decided to rape you or something?"

"You're right, Choua," she answered. "But you know what? I'm tired of talking about it. Let's go look at makeup before we have to go home."

I got home later than 9:30 because we had fun trying on makeup and forgot about the time. I ran almost all the way home, which was okay because it kept me warm. I came in as quietly as I could, but my mother saw me. She didn't say anything, but she looked sad and hurt. I would feel better if she beat me or something. I know she wonders if I am going to be like Mai when I get a little older. I hope she doesn't think I was doing anything bad. Oh crap, I bet she noticed the makeup. That means she knows I wasn't at the library.

I should go and explain to her and apologize, but I have so much homework to do. I'm going to be up until midnight. Maybe I'll talk to her in the morning.

Friday, November 24

Well, it's Hmong New Year tomorrow, and Mai is still at the detention center. Her court date was changed because the judge got sick. She's been there for more than three weeks now. The secretary keeps calling me out of class to ask when Mai is coming back to school. There's a school at the juvenile detention center, but I don't know what they do there. I wonder if she'll pass eleventh grade. If she doesn't, that means we'll be in the same grade next year. That would really suck.

I've only seen Mai that one time since she ran away. Truthfully, it's better at home without her. I'm just trying to have fun these days. School is good, and Leticia doesn't pick on me anymore now that I hang out with Frankie. Even though Frankie's different than the rest of us, we don't care. It's interesting to hear her stories, and find out what non-Asian people do. I still don't like black kids, but I like Frankie all right. She's the bomb.

Because it's Hmong New Year we're partying all weekend. I can't wait until tomorrow. We're going to get up early and go to the Riverfront Center as soon as it opens. Dad didn't let us go tonight because he was working. Of course, Mom or Ger could have driven us, but Dad always has to be the big boss. He told us, "If I can't go, nobody's going." I watched MTV most of the night with Ka to get over being mad at him. Oh well, I'm going to go to bed now. It's really late and I want to be wide awake for tomorrow.

Sunday, November 26

I got up early so I could write everything that happened yesterday. It was the most exciting day of my whole life! We're going back to the Riverfront Center in a couple of hours for the last day of Hmong New Year. Today they're going to crown Miss Hmong New Year. Also, Bee and her cousins are going to perform a Hmong traditional dance. They've been practicing for the last month. I feel a little jealous because I'm no good at singing or dancing. I don't know what I'm good at. Maybe writing?

Yesterday we all got up early so we could get to the Riverfront Center as soon as it opened. Even Ger. The little kids and my mom got dressed up in traditional Hmong clothes. I couldn't decide what to do. I wanted to wear my American clothes, but I knew Dad would make me wear my traditional outfit. Ka and I decided to wear our Hmong clothes to the Riverfront Centre, and change into jeans and some platforms when we got there. The platforms kill my feet, but they look really cool. We put a little glitter and mascara on our eyes after we got changed, and last night Ka and I painted each other's nails a kind of blue, sparkly color so we looked really tight. I just prayed Dad wouldn't catch us, but there were so many thousands of people there, I didn't think he would.

Ka and I walked around for a long time looking for our friends, but there were so many people that we had no luck. Man, there are a lot of pretty Hmong girls! I felt kind of ugly around some of them. There were a bunch of girls in their traditional clothes playing catch with some boys in the big ballroom. Maybe some of you don't know about that tradition. You throw a ball back and forth with a boy. It's kind of like flirting. All the pretty girls have crowds of boys around them. It's supposed to kind of romantic, but it isn't romantic like you see in the movies or anything.

Like I told you, most Hmong girls I know aren't allowed to go on dates. (Not that anyone has ever asked me.) I feel like I'm in a culture clash. Everywhere I look kids are holding hands or kissing in the hallway. I don't want to throw some stupid ball—I want to go on dates and fall in love! It pisses me off that I'm not allowed to do that. Maybe I could do it without my dad finding out, but then I would be just like Mai. Normally, I don't let myself think about this very much, but this amazing thing happened yesterday...

While Ka and I were searching for our friends, I ran into Ku. Remember I told you about him at the beginning of this journal? He's also in tenth grade at Como, and his locker is just down the hall from mine. We're in the same social studies class. I think he knows I have a crush on him because my friends used to push me in front of him and giggle. How juvenile can you get? Then a few months ago Bee wrote him a note that said, "Choua Vang thinks you're the bomb." She gave it to his friend, Seng, and he gave it to Ku. When I found out, I was so embarrassed I nearly died! I didn't speak to Bee for days after that.

That was at the beginning of the school year and nothing has happened since. Ku never talked to me. Not one word. I can't blame him, but I can't even look at him without getting red. Then yesterday, there he was standing beside a booth selling Hmong music. He was with his friends, laughing and acting cool. They were wearing baggy pants and baseball caps. I saw him first, and even though he didn't see me, I blushed.

Ka asked me, "Who are those cute boys?"

"Come on Ka, let's get out of here," I said. I wanted him to notice me, but it was too hard to just stand there and see what would happen. But at that exact minute, Ku turned around and saw me. He smiled right away – a nice, slow, shy smile that made me feel like ice cream melting.

"Hey Choua, whassup?"

He knew my name!

I tried to act real cool. "Not much," I said. "How about you?"

"Just looking around," he said.

At that moment, Bee and her sister, Tria, showed up. Bee looked really surprised to see me talking to Ku.

Then Ku said, "Hey, we're going to watch the Miss Hmong pageant. You wanna join us?"

I swear, my heart stopped beating!

"Yeah, I guess so," I said, and I flung my hair behind my shoulders the way Mai does. Mai says I shouldn't act too interested if I like a boy. She says you should keep them guessing.

We all went and watched the Miss Hmong New Year pageant together, and *Ku and I sat next to each other*! It seemed like he let all his friends go ahead of him so he would be at the end of the row, and then Bee pushed me forward so I would be sitting next to him. I don't know if he wanted it that way or not, but it made me feel all tingly and nervous. I made sure that my hands were in my lap and I never looked at him. I felt all sweaty and gross. I popped some gum in my mouth because I had just eaten some *qaub* (that's papaya salad for those of you who don't know) with Ka. I was scared I might have bad breath.

We sat and watched without saying anything. Someone told me that the bride price for Miss Hmong New Year is more than ten thousand dollars. That's more than double the usual price. The contestants all came out in traditional Hmong clothing and bowed to the audience. Most of them were really pretty, but one girl was kind of fat and another one had a lot of pimples on her face. I don't think I could ever enter. I know I'm not pretty enough, and besides, I think it's kind of stupid. I don't think girls should have to prove anything by the way they look.

After the traditional part, they all came back wearing long dresses like you would wear to the prom. They didn't look like the same girls. Some of the dresses were really sexy. I could hear two old Hmong men saying it was terrible, and that they should only be allowed to wear Hmong clothing.

Bee looked at me and said, "I think they look great. Those old Hmong men don't know what they're talking about! I'd rather wear one of those dresses than a stupid Hmong costume."

I don't know about that. I'm kind of proud of my traditional clothes. I guess I like wearing American clothes better, but I don't think Hmong clothes are stupid.

Each girl had to give a little speech about herself. All of them did it in Hmong except for one girl who talked in Hmong and English.

Lots of them said they were going to be doctors or businesswomen. One said she was going to be a pilot. A bunch said they wanted to be teachers. It surprised me that they had such high goals. I wonder if they were just making it up or if they really meant it. I bet most of them will be married in the next year or two and turn into baby-making machines.

Then I thought of Mai stuck at the juvenile detention center in Wausau. She loves Hmong New Year. It's like Christmas to her so I bet she's in a nasty mood this weekend. I wouldn't want to go anywhere near her. She's probably going to bite somebody's head off!

The whole time we were watching, I could tell Ku was kind of nervous. He looked over at me a bunch of times, but I pretended not to notice. My heart was racing! He's so handsome and cool. I have no idea why he'd be interested in little ol' me. He could get someone way better.

While we were watching, Ku talked with his friends and laughed a lot, but he didn't say anything to me. I felt kind of disappointed, but I didn't talk to him, either. After we had sat there for about 15 or 20 minutes he said, "We're going to go check out the food. Maybe I'll catch you later."

Did that mean he wanted to see me later or was he just being polite? I wanted to beg him to stay, but that would have looked desperate.

So I said, "Yeah, okay. I'll catch you later."

I felt disappointed and excited all at the same time. I really just wanted to sit beside him forever on those hard cold seats.

The boys shuffled past us, and then suddenly Ku turned around and said, "Hey, maybe we could meet at school some time."

That was the HAPPIEST moment of my life. I keep running it through my head again and again and again. He really likes me!

"Sure," I said. "That would be cool." I sounded really calm and relaxed, but what I was really thinking was, "Oh, my God! I can't believe one of the cutest boys at school wants to meet me!

Well, I've got to go. We're leaving for the last day of Hmong New Year. My family is already piling into the van. Maybe I'll see Ku again today. Oh my God, I hope so!

Monday, November 27

I didn't write after Hmong New Year finished yesterday because I was too depressed. I looked around for Ku all day on Sunday, but I never saw him. There were thousands and thousands of people there so I shouldn't have been so surprised. The whole time I felt like I was going to be sick because I wanted to see him so much. So Sunday wasn't so great, but I just keep remembering Saturday and I feel better.

But something else happened that was kind of bad. I didn't find out until after I got home, but Ka's friend, Zoua, saw it happen. It's about Ger. He met some of his friends at the entrance, and when they tried to get in, they were turned away. They were wearing big baggy pants and red bandannas. There were signs all over the Riverfront Center that said there were no weapons or gang clothes allowed.

I really don't think they were planning any trouble. I mean, Ger might be in a gang, but the more I think about it, the more I think it can't be a bad gang. There must be good gangs too. It's probably just a bunch of guys who hang out and drink beer once in a while. I just don't think Ger is looking for trouble. He's too smart.

When they weren't allowed in, they said, "Hey look, we're not here to cause trouble. We're just here to have fun," and stuff like that, but the attendants still wouldn't let them in. So then the guys got really pissed off and tried to start a fight.

There are a lot of police at Hmong New Year because they're worried about gang violence (a kid was shot in the head at Hmong New Year in Green Bay last year). They came right away and broke up the fight. Nothing happened, but the police told Ger and his friends to leave or they'd be arrested. That's so stupid! Who cares what they wear? They were just there for a good time like the rest of us.

The trouble is, Ger didn't come home last night. I stayed up really late waiting for him, but he never showed. Sometimes he crawls in through his bedroom window, but he didn't do that either. I checked. Where does he sleep? What does he do all night? I've made up my mind that I'm going to ask him next time I see him.

The only thing that's helping me feel better is thinking about Ku. I told Trisha all about what happened at New Year. She didn't go because she's not Hmong. Mostly only Hmong and curious white people go. She said I should talk to Ku when I see him in the hallway, and say something like, "Hmong New Year was cool, huh?" just to start a conversation. But I'm so nervous!

I know I shouldn't even be thinking about Ku. My dad would have a fit if he knew what I was thinking. He'd lock me in the house and never let me go out again!

I feel really confused about this. Mai is stuck in juvenile detention center because she doesn't want to marry some stranger when she's sixteen. All this time, I've been thinking that she needs to respect Dad and our culture and accept the fact that we don't do things the way white people do. But now I feel kind of like I'm on her side. Why *can't* I go out with a guy? Why should my dad tell me what to do? Some

Hmong girls are allowed to date if the boy visits the girl at her house, but my dad would never even allow that. Why does he have to act this way? We're in America now. We need to change with the times! All I really know is that I want to be with Ku. I want even more than that. I want him to put his arms around me and ... I won't let myself think about it. Ger and Mai are both screwing up their lives because they won't act Hmong. I'm just going to try and forget about Ku and focus on my schoolwork and friends. Yeah, right!

Okay, for this minute I won't think about Ku. Oops, I just thought about him. Okay, starting now. Crap, I did it again. How am I supposed to stop? I think I'm in love...

Thursday, December 7

Mai came home yesterday. She finally had her court date after waiting more than a month. Mom and Dad drove out to Wausau for the hearing, and to pick her up. She came in to the house ahead of them, slammed the door right in their faces, and walked into our bedroom like she owned the place. It felt like a cold wind blowing into the house, like winter had come.

"It's a pigpen in here," were her first words. "What's the matter with you all? You could have at least cleaned the room for me." She threw her bag down on the bed and started unpacking. Her breathing was heavy, as if she'd just finished chopping wood. I could tell she was angry. My sisters and I just sat on our beds watching her. We didn't know what to say. She felt like a stranger.

"So what happened at court?" I finally asked.

"Nothing!" she hissed. "The judge said if I ran away again, he'd send me to a group home. Then he let me go. It was a stupid waste of time! I mean, I spent a whole month in the juvenile detention center, and it was all over in less than three minutes!"

It sounded like she was upset that the judge had let her off.

Actually, I think she was upset that she had to come home. I bet she liked the juvenile detention center better than here. At least there she could hang out with other bad kids like herself.

"Are you happy to be home?" Nou asked in a small, scared voice.

"Are you kidding? I'm getting out of here as soon as I can! Don't be surprised if you wake up one morning and I'm not here. Don't be surprised if I never come back."

Mai looked different than she had a month ago. Not ugly exactly, but there was something hard about her. It was like all that anger had taken away her soft prettiness and replaced it with a stone statue. I didn't like being in the same room with her. It made me uncomfortable.

Mai finally noticed that we were all miserable and feeling scared. She got soft for a second and said, "It's nice to see you all again. I missed you. But you better not have worn any of my clothes!"

Ka and I had worn her clothes almost every day, but we were careful to clean them and hang them all up before she got home.

"Are you kidding?" I said. "You'd kill us!"

Then we laughed and we all felt a little bit better.

Wednesday, December 13

We're all waiting for Ku to talk to me. It's almost Christmas vacation, and not a damn thing has happened.

Frankie says, "Girl, just go and talk to him. He likes you and you like him!"

Bee says, "Just play it cool. Don't act like you like him. Pretend you don't notice him." She actually talks to her dad about dating. He's a lot more modern than my dad. I think she'll probably be able to marry for love. Bee is brave. I could never do that with my dad. I'd be too embarrassed, and he'd probably beat me. I've known Bee since third grade, and she is always the leader. I think she will do something important with her life someday. She's just that kind of person.

Trisha's advice is, "Go for it. You know he likes you so you have nothing to lose. Just go and talk to him!" Of course, Trisha has already kissed a senior. She's much more experienced than the rest of us. None of us has ever kissed anyone or even held hands. Since Trisha kissed Ken, it's kind of like she's the bad girl now, but also the experienced, cool one in the group. I was only tagging along like a baby sister.

Frankie made us promise we'd never smoke pot again. She said, "It makes you stupid and lazy. My brother smokes pot all the time and he don't ever do nothing but sit in front of the TV and drink beer. Swear on your granny's grave that you'll never do it again!"

We swore we wouldn't. I agree with her. It *was* stupid, and I'm not going to do it again. She doesn't need to worry about me. But back to what I was talking about...

WHY WON'T KU TALK TO ME?

It's already two weeks later and he hasn't even said hi. I see him in the hallway and in social studies class, but he doesn't even look at me. I don't get it! I'm starting to wonder if he talked to me at Hmong New Year on a dare. Maybe he doesn't like me at all. Maybe he just wants to embarrass me.

Trisha says, "Boys are funny. They pretend they're not interested because they think it's cool." Actually, that's what I've been doing, too, but if we both keep pretending, we'll never talk to each other again!

After school, we all went to Trisha's house and tried on her mom's makeup and did each other's hair. We laughed and laughed, and ate ice cream with chocolate sauce. Life is easier without boys.

Monday, December 18

When I got home from school today, Ger was sitting in the living room. He's hardly ever around so I thought, "Now's my chance to finally talk to him." I felt a little shy because we hardly ever talk anymore, and I didn't know if he had time for his kid sister.

"Hey," I said.

"Whassup, Sis?" he asked.

"Nothing much. How about you?"

"I'm just waiting around for some of my friends."

"You're always out with your friends," I said. "What do you guys do?"

"Nothing much," he answered. "Just hang out. Same stuff you do with your friends."

"I know you're in a gang," I said. I just blurted it out because I didn't know how to fit it into the conversation.

"Yeah? So what?" Ger answered. He looked kind of nervous, and maybe a little embarrassed. It was hard to tell.

"I just want to know why. It's so dangerous."

"You know, Choua, it's like this," he said. He sat up a little straighter and his voice got kind of angry, though I knew he wasn't angry at me. "You go to school, your teachers yell at you. You come home, your parents yell at you. So you just end up with your home-boys on the streets."

"I still don't get it," I said. "What do you guys do?"

"We mostly just hang out and drink beer, smoke some pot. Some gangs are really into fighting and shit, but we keep a pretty low profile. I'm not interested in hurting anyone."

"Do you steal stuff, like when Mai and those dudes stole the car?"

"Listen Choua," he said, "I don't think we should be talking about this kind of stuff. You're too young."

"I am not!" I said. "I'm tired of not knowing what's going on. Just tell me. I'm not a baby!"

"All right, all right, but you can't tell Mom and Dad. Promise?"

"Yeah, I promise," I said.

This was the most Ger and I had talked together in years. It was perfect timing because my brothers and sisters were watching cartoons and my parents weren't home from work yet. As usual, I didn't know where Mai was.

"Okay, I'll tell you. But listen to me, Choua," he said, looking at me real serious-like, "My gang is like my family. We're really close. But that doesn't mean you should join a gang. They can get you in a lot of trouble. Promise me you won't get into a gang, okay, Sis?"

"I won't. I promise. Just tell me." That was the second time I promised.

"Well," he began, "I usually get up like I'm going to school, and then I meet my homeboys and we go cruising and shit. Then when it's time for school to be over we come home. The school probably phones to say I'm absent, but nobody's ever home. If any mail comes from school, I take it before Mom and Dad see it. They can't read it anyway."

"Don't you ever go to school?" I asked, remembering how nervous I was when I skipped out with Trisha just once.

"Oh sure, I go just enough so I don't get kicked out."

"So how do you get by?"

"I just take the easiest courses so I don't have to study. I'm not trying to get a scholarship or anything. I just want to graduate."

"But you're so smart!" I said. "Don't you want to go to college or something?"

"Get real," he said, looking really mad. "Poor people don't get to go to college, and Hmong kids almost never go. I'll just get a job on an assembly line or something."

"I don't get it," I said. "Don't you want to do more than that?"

"Nah," he said. "Life is short and then you die."

I couldn't believe the way he was talking. It didn't sound like my brother Ger who used to work so hard and be so kind. Actually, he sounded a lot like Mai.

"So do you ever steal stuff?" I asked.

"Yeah, sure, but we don't hurt nobody. Rich people don't need all that shit anyway. They should share some of it with us."

I was shocked. "But what if you get caught?" I asked.

"If I get caught, I get caught," he said. "So far I haven't. Anyway, I don't steal all that much, just enough to get by."

Then I asked the question I was most curious about. "Do Mom and Dad know you're in a gang?"

"I don't know about Mom," he answered, "but Dad knows. Do you know what he does? He yells at me for being in a gang and tells me how stupid I am, and that I'm going to get myself killed. Then he has the nerve to come and ask me for money. He knows I got it from stealing and he still asks for it. What a jerk!"

That was another surprise. Why would Dad ask for dirty money? He must really need it. I knew we were poor, but I didn't know we needed money that badly.

I changed the subject. "Sometimes you're gone all night, Ger," I said. "It freaks me out. Where do you go?"

"You sure have a lot of questions, don't you?" he said. "What are you doing, writing a book?"

I kind of blushed when he said that, but I didn't say anything.

"We usually sleep in one of the homeboy's basements, and then sneak out before anyone wakes up. Sometimes we break into people's garages and sleep there or we find old abandoned houses. There are lots of places to sleep. As long as you've got enough blankets and beer in your body to keep warm, you're fine."

I just sat there and stared at him. "This is my brother," I thought. "This is what he does." If this is what happens to people who are in gangs, I don't want to be in one. His shirt was all wrinkled and stained, and his hair was all slicked back and greasy. It looked like he hadn't slept in a long time. For the first time I saw that he had really changed. He wasn't my big brother Ger that I used to admire so much.

He saw me staring and said, "Get out of here, Sis. I'm tired of talking. Go do your homework so you can go to college. Maybe one person in this family will do something worthwhile."

So I came back here and wrote it all down so I won't forget. If I'm ever tempted to get into a gang, all I have to do is read this journal.

Sunday, December 24

Last week the only thing I could think about was Ku. Now I couldn't care less. Something has happened that makes all that seem stupid and meaningless. My brother was shot. Even as I write those words, my hands start to shake. It's just so hard to believe. I'll tell you from the beginning. It might make me feel better to write about it.

The other night I was watching TV with my sisters when the doorbell rang. I went to get it and there was a policeman standing there. It kind of scared me. At first I thought he was there to take away Mai again. I wanted to tell her to hide in a closet or something.

"Is this the Vang residence?" he asked.

"Yes. What do you want?" I said.

"Is your mom or dad around?"

I went to get my parents. I stayed in case they needed help understanding, but really I just wanted to know what was going on.

"Mr. and Mrs. Vang, do you have a son named Ger?"

My parents looked at each other, really scared-like, and then they both nodded.

"Is he in trouble?" my father asked.

"He's in the hospital, Mr. Vang. He's been shot."

My heart stopped beating. I didn't think of anything for the next few seconds. It was like being caught in the middle of a tornado. I've heard that everything is perfectly still right in the center even though wind is blowing all around you at a hundred miles an hour.

And then the tornado hit. Ger shot? In the hospital? Was he alive? Was he okay? How did it happen? I had a million questions, but I couldn't seem to open my mouth.

My father asked the question we all wanted to know. "Is my son dead?"

"No, Sir, he's not," the policeman said. "He's still alive, but he could die. You and your wife need to come with me right now. You can follow me to the hospital. Go and get your coats. I'll wait by the squad car."

In a few seconds my parents and the policeman were gone, leaving the rest of us staring at each other in the living room with nothing to say. The lights on the plastic Christmas tree were blinking on and off, reminding us that this was supposed to be the happiest time of the year. For white folks maybe.

Mai started to cry, and then so did Ka and Nou. The boys just walked around the room looking worried. The babies played quietly. They had no idea what was going on. Nobody knew what to say or what to do.

You never know what you will do when you hear the worst news of your life. I guess a lot of people cry or scream or something. I went to the kitchen and started cleaning up. I put away all the dishes from supper and then I swept the floor and scrubbed it. After a while, Ka and Mai came in and joined me. It just felt better to be doing something. Anything. It made the waiting less scary.

I think we must have cleaned the house for hours. The house hasn't been so clean since the day we moved in. It was way past midnight when my parents came back. The little kids were sleeping on the sofa and the floor, but the rest of us were wide-awake. I felt like I would never sleep again.

I think we were all too scared to say anything so we just waited. I could tell my mother had been crying. They came in and crumpled up onto the sofa.

"Ger was shot in the back," my father said in Hmong. "The bullet is still there, close to his spine. The doctors want to do an operation to take it out. Right now he can't move his body. It's *tuag duav*." That means *dead* in English because we don't have the word paralyzed in the Hmong language.

I was so tired that it took a minute for me to understand the words. He couldn't move his hands or feet? How can you do anything if you can't move? All these thoughts were whirling through my head like rain on a stormy night.

"Is he going to be okay?" Mai whispered.

My father sighed. "I don't know," he said. "We have to wait and see."

I had just spent the whole night waiting, and that seemed like forever.

"How long will we have to wait?" I asked.

"As long as it takes," he said.

Monday, December 25

Today was Christmas day, but of course, no one felt like celebrating. The gifts, wrapped in newspaper, are still lying under the tree. They look really awful, not like the beautiful, shiny packages tied with bows that other kids have. Plus, there are just a few of them, not even enough for all the kids. No one really cares anyway. They're probably just old clothes my mom bought from the thrift store, or maybe some socks.

After my father told us what happened last night, we all went to our rooms and pretended to go to sleep. I hardly slept at all. I kept waking up and thinking about Ger. It was better being asleep because my real life is a nightmare now.

My parents were in the kitchen when I got up at around ten o'clock.

"Do you know anything else?" I asked.

"No, we're going to the hospital now. You can come along if you want," my father told me. I knew there would probably be an interpreter, but just in case, I decided to go with them. To tell the truth, I didn't really want to go because I was scared to see Ger. I didn't know what he would look like. Hospitals freak me out.

"Hurry up and get dressed," my mother told me. "We're leaving in five minutes."

We drove to Region's Hospital and went to a room with a big number seven on the door. I think they called it the trauma room. It's a room for people who need to be watched very closely and who are still very sick. Hospitals smell funny, and you never know what kind of horrible thing you're going to see, like a dead body or something. There were decorations all over and a big Christmas tree beside the elevator. I'm sure they were trying to make the hospital cheerful and Christmassy, but it didn't work. The decorations just made everything around them seem even more depressing. Walking down the hallway to his room was one of the longest walks I ever took. I was scared of what I would see on the other side.

There was Ger in bed hooked up to all kinds of machines and stuff. It was horrible to look at. I wanted to run out of the room and back to my old life. But he was awake and he was looking at me so I felt like I had to say something.

"Hi Ger," I said. "Merry Christmas."

As soon as I said that, I knew it was the stupidest thing anyone could ever say. You don't wish someone who's just been shot Merry Christmas!

He looked at me and blinked. It looked like he kind of tried to smile, but I'm not sure.

My mom sat beside his bed and held his hand. My dad just stood in the corner. Nobody knew what to say. I didn't know if he could talk or not. He didn't seem like he was very wide awake.

All that silence felt like a waterfall rushing around me. I wanted to scream. Anything was better than the terrible silence so I decided I had to say something. I had no idea what to say, but I just opened my mouth and the words came out. "Do you remember how you used to help me with my times tables in elementary school?"

Ger looked at me and nodded. "Yeah, kid, I do," he said.

I breathed a sigh of relief. At least I knew he could talk.

"Thanks," I said. "That was cool."

"Don't mention it," he said and then he smiled a little.

The doctor came in at that moment and told my mom and dad to come into the hallway. I decided to stay with Ger. They could come and get me if they needed me to help interpret.

I felt a little closer to him now, and I was getting used to all the machines he was hooked up to so I decided to ask him what I really wanted to know.

"What happened, Ger?"

"I got shot, stupid. Can't you see?" He kind of smiled when he said that. It wasn't like he was trying to be mean.

"But why? I don't get it!"

"Are you sure you want to know?" he asked.

I took a deep breath and said, "Tell me."

"Well, me and my homeboys were out cruising last night. We weren't looking for any trouble. We were just killing time. We went to Mounds Park just to hang out and drink a few beers and listen to some music. We were in the parking lot when this car came speeding by and one of the homeboys from another gang stuck his gun out the window and started firing. We beat up one of their homeboys last week cuz he tried to steal one of our girls. I think he got some of my friends too. I'm not sure. Nobody will tell me anything around here. I didn't even know I'd been hit at first. I didn't feel anything. That was the problem. Suddenly I couldn't feel any pain. Nothing."

He closed his eyes. I didn't know if he was just tired or if it was hard telling the story. I was quiet. I could still hear the doctor talking in a soft voice outside the door.

Then he talked again. "Choua, I can't feel anything in my legs. Put your hand on my knee."

I reached out and touched his knee that was sticking up under the white hospital sheet.

"I can't feel it," he said.

I could see his eyes start to well up with tears.

"I'm scared, Choua," he said.

I didn't know what to say. I was scared too.

Sunday, January 7

Christmas vacation was the worst ever. All we did was sit around the house and watch TV and worry about Ger. I haven't even been writing because I'm just too depressed. Why bother? Thank God school starts tomorrow. At least I'll have something to keep my mind off my sucky life.

Monday, January 8

It was good to go back to school today and see my friends again. I only talked on the phone with them a few times over break. They didn't really knew what to say or do after I told them about Ger. It's funny how uncomfortable people get around a person when they find out bad news about you or your family. I mean, I'm still the same person I was before winter break, I just have a paralyzed brother now. They tried to act normal when they saw me this morning, but they were really careful, like I was a painting in a museum that they couldn't touch or get too close to. Nobody brought up Ku, even though I've been thinking about him a lot. It seems kind of wrong to even think about him with all the bad stuff that's going on.

I decided I needed to talk to someone who wouldn't be scared to talk about what's happening. Ms. Martinez and I used to talk a lot, but she's been pretty busy lately. She's getting married this year, and she's planning a big wedding. Even though she's busy, I decided that I needed to talk to her today. She's the only adult I can talk to, and there was so much on my mind I felt like I might blow up.

When I got to her room before class this morning, she was sitting at her computer. She looked up and smiled when I came in.

"Hi, Choua! I'm so glad to see you. I've missed talking to you lately."

I knew she really meant it. She's one of those people you feel really comfortable with, and you never need to worry that she doesn't like you or she's wishing you would go away. I get that feeling from most other adults.

"Do you have some time to talk?" I asked. "I really need to talk to you about some important stuff."

She looked at her watch and said, "Well, the rest of the kids will be coming in any minute now. Why don't we have lunch instead? I tell you what, I'll sign us out at the office, and we can walk around Como Lake. I'll get us some sandwiches and fruit to take along."

"Great," I said. I'd never been anywhere with a teacher. We agreed to meet at noon in her room. I felt pretty excited to be going out with her. How many teachers would do that for you?

We walked to the lake and sat on a park bench to eat. It was crisp and cold, but luckily, I got some money over Christmas vacation to buy a coat so I was warm enough except for my feet. I know I should wear boots, but they're just not cool. I was wearing my platform sneakers that made me slip and slide on the icy patches on the sidewalk.

After we chewed on our pb and j sandwiches for a few minutes, Ms. M. asked, "So Choua, what do you want to talk about?"

I got straight to the point and said, "I don't know if you heard about that gang shooting over Christmas vacation. The boy who was shot and paralyzed is my brother, Ger."

Ms. Martinez almost dropped her sandwich. "Oh my God! That was your brother? Choua, that's terrible. I read about it in the newspaper, but I had no idea! Is he all right?"

I told her about my visit with him and that he couldn't move. Then I told her about Mai running away from home. As she listened, I saw her wipe away some tears with her napkin. It was sweet of her to cry like that. I mean, it's not *her* family.

"How are you dealing with all this, Choua? It must be pretty awful for you," she asked me as we ate stared at the ice shacks on the frozen lake.

"It totally is," I said. "I think about Ger every second, and I'm really worried about Mai, too. I feel like I can't concentrate on my schoolwork or even spend time with my friends. I don't want to do anything. I always watch TV these days because I don't have to think when I'm doing that. I haven't even been keeping up with."

"That's pretty common, Choua," she said. "Most people going through hard times want to escape and not think about their problems."

Then she put her hand on my arm, and asked, "Choua, how can I help?"

I could see that she really meant it, but I didn't know what to say. I wasn't sure. I thought for a minute and then it came to me.

"I just need someone to talk to," I said. "I feel a little better when I can talk to someone who will really listen to me. It helps me sort out my feelings."

Ms. Martinez smiled and said, "You know, Choua, I want to be here for you. Anytime you want to talk, I'll be happy to listen." Then she got a pen and piece of notepaper out of her purse and started writing something.

"Here's my phone number," she said. "Anytime you want to talk, please call. If I'm not home, leave a message and I'll call you back."

I looked at her with surprise.

"Really," she said. "I mean it!"

I took the paper, folded it up carefully and put it in my wallet. I'd feel kind of silly calling her at home, but you never know.

I felt a lot better after talking to her. She didn't give me any advice or anything. She just listened. I appreciate that. It really helped, in the same way writing in this journal helps. It's kind of like folding your clean laundry when it comes out of the dryer, and then putting everything away, giving all your clothes a home. It feels good to know they're in the right place.

Tuesday, January 16

Sorry I haven't written in about a week. A lot's been going on. I don't have the energy to go into all the details, but I'll tell you quickly. Ger is still in the hospital. They did an operation to remove the bullet from the area around his spine, and they don't know if he'll still be paralyzed or not. The doctors say it's too early to tell because it's still really swollen in that area. I've only seen him once since the operation because he's on a lot of drugs and the doctors say he has to rest a lot.

I found out that one of Ger's friends died the other day. He was shot in the head during the drive-by shooting, and he's been on life-support ever since. I guess he was a vegetable, like his brain had completely shut down, and the doctors finally persuaded his parents to pull the plug. His name was Meng. I don't know him so I don't feel that sad. I mean, I'm sad, but at least I don't have to feel terrible that someone I know died. I don't even know if Ger knows about it yet.

The other bad thing is that Ger's gang went out the day after the shooting to get revenge, and they killed two guys from the other gang. The police caught them yesterday, and now they're in jail. How stupid can you get! The whole thing is just making me madder and madder. All this killing is crazy. It's like a bad movie. I just want to say, "Wake up, you assholes, look at what you're doing. Do you all want to die?"

Mai hasn't been around very much lately. She's sneaking out again now that Mom and Dad don't have time to watch her so closely. That makes me mad, too. She sees what happened to Ger, but she's still hanging out with her homeboys. What's the matter with her? I've stopped talking to her because she's so stupid. If she wants to ruin her life, that's her business.

The more I think about it all, the more I know I just want to live my own life and do my own thing. So what if everyone thinks I'm just a quiet little Hmong girl! Maybe my parents think I'm just going to get married and have babies. Maybe my teachers think I'll just do okay in school, and then I'll get a job and get married or something. But I know the truth! I, Choua Vang, am going to be SOMEBODY! I am going to graduate and go to college and write books and get famous.

Someday people will see me and say, "Oh look, isn't that Choua Vang? She wrote a best selling book. We used to think she was just a little ol' Hmong girl. We never really even noticed her at school. No one ever dreamed she would do anything special with her life. Look at her now. She's rich and famous. I'm so jealous!"

That's how I'm going to get everyone back—by becoming somebody important. Nobody is going to tell me what I can or cannot do.

Not the Hmong. Not the Americans. I am going to do exactly what I want to do starting NOW! Here's my promise:

On January 16, 2001, I, Choua Vang, make the solemn promise that I will make my dreams come true, and I will do what I want to do, and not what others think I should do. I will always follow my heart.

Signed, Choua Vang.

(Did you notice it's signed with my own blood? I poked my finger with a pin to show the world how serious I am.)

Thursday, January 18

I've been waiting so long for Ku to come and talk to me, that I finally decided it was time for me to talk to him. That's part of my new life now. I do what I want. So what if I get turned down? Sure, it'll hurt my feelings, but I've felt enough pain lately not to worry about a little more. Besides, Frankie says, there are plenty of fish in the sea. I think that means there are lots of other boys in the world to fall in love with. She's right.

I've been writing all over my notebooks for months *Choua Loves Ku*, but today was the day to find out if *he* loved *me*. I told my friends to stand a little way down the hallway so they could listen in while I waited for him by his locker.

When I saw him coming, all cute in his cargo pants, Tommy Hilfiger tee shirt and split, spiky hair, I got nervous all of a sudden and wanted to run away. But I didn't. I remembered my promise to myself.

I think he was a little surprised to see me standing at his locker.

"Hi Ku," I said. "Whassup?"

"Not much," he said. "How about you?"

I put my hands in my pockets because they were so sweaty. My face felt fevery hot, but I was excited kind of like the feeling you get when you're on the top of the first hill on a roller coaster and you're just about to go down.

"I just thought I'd come by and say hello, that's all," I said. "We talked about meeting at school some time and then we never did."

I couldn't believe I was standing there and saying that. I have never been so brave in my whole, entire life. I was braver than a bullfighter with a giant bull running straight at his red cape.

Ku blushed, like he was embarrassed. I was glad. He *should* be embarrassed, I thought to myself. How dare he not talk to me when he said he would? What a jerk! Suddenly I felt really angry. Why was I wasting my time with a guy like this anyway? I didn't care what happened after that. Then I wasn't nervous anymore.

"I'm real sorry, Choua," he said, all sweet-like.

Suddenly I didn't feel so angry anymore.

"I guess I'm kind of shy," he said. "I really wanted to talk to you. Everyday I tell myself that I'm going to, and then I chicken out."

Now it was my time to blush. Oh my God, did that mean he still liked me?

"Really?" I asked.

"Yeah, really," he answered. "I'm really glad you came to my locker. I don't know if I'd ever have the guts to talk to you. I mean, you're so pretty and cool. I didn't think you could like someone like me."

That's the stupidest thing I've ever heard in my life. Number one, I don't think I'm very pretty at all. Number two, I'm not cool. Bee, Trisha and Frankie are my only friends in the world. Number three, what did he mean *someone like me?* He is only the cutest guy in the whole entire school! If he doesn't know that, he's never looked in a mirror!

After that I didn't know what to say. My mind was just spinning in circles. Also, I felt kind of shy all of a sudden. We both stood there kind of stupid-like until Bee came over and rescued me.

"Come on, Choua," she said. "Let's go have lunch." And then she looked over at Ku as if she had just noticed him and said, "Oh hi, Ku."

"See you later," I said and smiled at him.

"Yeah, I'll see you in the morning," he said, and he gave me the cutest smile that made me warm all the way down to my toes.

So right now I am cuddled up in bed feeling JUST FINE! When we turn the lights off in a few minutes, I might practice kissing with the pillow. (I'm going to take that sentence out before anyone ever reads this. How embarrassing!)

Friday, January 19

Dad just came home and told us Ger can move his legs now, and he is going to walk again. The doctors say it will take a long, long time and he may never be completely normal, but he has some feeling in his legs. I'm so happy I feel like I could fly.

Dad says I can go visit him next weekend. I'm going to tell him exactly what I think: that if he doesn't get out of the gang after this he's the stupidest person on the whole earth and he's not going to be my brother anymore. I wasn't going to say anything if he was paralyzed because that would be too mean. Since he isn't, I'm really going to tell him. It's the new me. I say what I think. I do what I want.

Now maybe I can stop thinking about him for a while and think about my own GREAT LIFE! Do you remember how Ku said, "See you in the morning" yesterday? When I got to my locker this morning, he was standing there waiting for me.

"Hey," I said. "What are you doing here?"

"I told you I'd see you in the morning," he answered.

"I didn't think you'd really show up."

"Well, here I am," he said. "You look nice today."

I blushed. We didn't really know what to say to each other. I hope it gets a little easier.

"Thanks," I mumbled, "but no I don't."

"Yes, you do," he said.

So we talked like that for a while. Of course I remember every word, but it sounds kind of stupid when I write it down.

But then he shuffled his feet and looked all embarrassed, like he wanted to ask me something, but he didn't know how to say it. Then he just blurted it out, "Wanna go to the Valentines dance with me?"

Oh my God, I can still hardly believe it! I didn't think I would ever go to a dance, and I don't know if I can really go. Dad doesn't let us go out at night, especially if there are boys and girls together. But if he doesn't let me go this time, I think I'm going to die. Who am I kidding? He won't let me go in a million years!

I HAVE TO GO! I HAVE TO GO! I WILL GO! I'll find a way. If Dad doesn't let me, I'll just have to sneak out. Maybe I won't ask him at all. That's the answer! I'll just pretend I'm going to Trisha's house for night. Her mom let's her do anything so that won't be a problem. Oh, I'm so glad I've got this all figured out. Writing really helps me. I was worried about this all day, but as soon as I started writing about it, the answer came. Cool!

So back to my story: Ku couldn't even look at me after he asked me to the dance. I pretended like it was no big deal. I just said, "Sure. That would be cool." Bee says I should have played hard-to-get and told him I'd think about it. She says he made me wait so long that I should make him wait too! Maybe she's right, but I was just so excited that I had to say yes.

So it's been a great, great day. The only small thing that is bugging me is that it's after midnight and Mai isn't home yet. Stupid girl.

Monday, January 22

My mom made me pay the bills tonight. I wrote all these checks for gas and water and rent and cable. I hope we have enough money to pay them all. Mom didn't tell me how much money was in the account. She just said to write the checks and she would sign them. It was a lot of money.

I'm just a kid. I don't think I should have that kind of responsibility. Just because my older brother and sister are in trouble, I have to do all their stupid chores now. That pisses me off. I also had to bring the check to the landlord and tell him, "I'm sorry it's late this month."

Mai should be doing this, but she's too selfish to help. All she wants to do is hang out with her homeboys and smoke pot and drink beer. God, I hate her. Because of her, I had to miss school yesterday because my brother and sister, Pao and Ia, needed to go to the doctor, and Mom needed me to tell the doctor what was wrong. Youa couldn't take them because she had other plans for the day. I know my mom is trying, but she should just learn English so I don't have to do all her dirty work. I know she's busy, but she's been living in this country long enough! She's going to classes now, but why is it taking her so much longer to learn English than it took us kids? I guess that's not fair. I mean, I've been going to school for 11 years, counting kindergarten.

Anyway, today I am pissed off about being Hmong. It's too much work and there are too many expectations. When do I just get to be a kid and do normal kid things? All day long at school I'm an American. Then the minute I walk in the door I'm Hmong. Sometimes I feel like I'm two different people and I don't know which one is right. It would be much easier if I was just a white kid in America. At least I wouldn't be confused all the time.

Which reminds me: there's a new club starting at school called the International Club. Kids from other cultures get to know each other and do fun stuff together. Bee and Trisha and Frankie and I decided to join. Trisha said she thought it was bad that we didn't have any white friends, and Frankie reminded me that we didn't have any African American friends either. I don't know if I want any black friends other than Frankie. I know they can't be *all* bad, but I bet most Hmong people feel the same way that I do. Oh well, it's the new me so I'm going to go to the club and see what happens.

The only bright spot today was thinking about Ku and how we'll be close-dancing in a few weeks. Oh my God, I don't even know how to dance!

Tuesday, January 23

Today as I was putting my books in my locker before lunch, Ku showed up.

"Hey, wanna have lunch with me?" he asked.

For the first time I felt like we were girlfriend and boyfriend and it made me *sooo* happy!

"Sure," I said casually. "Just let me tell my friends."

Lunch is really short, just twenty-five minutes, but today is the longest we've ever been together. As we were walking down to the cafeteria he said, "Hey, I heard about your brother. I'm really sorry."

I was surprised. "Who told you?" I asked.

"Everyone knows," he said. "It's big news when there's a gang shooting. It's been in the paper for weeks."

We don't get a newspaper, and I guess I was so busy worrying that I never thought that other people might know it was my brother who was shot. No wonder people have been nice to me lately. How stupid can I be?

Ku has some good friends like Tong and Seng and Vang, but I don't think they're in a gang. I'm going to watch him real closely just to make sure. There's no way I'm going to go out with someone who's in a gang no matter how in love I am!

We went to the pop machine to buy a couple of Mountain Dews. Leticia and her friends were standing there. As soon as I saw them I wanted to turn around and walk away. But I didn't. "It's the new me," I reminded myself. "I'm not going to let them keep me from getting a drink." Besides, I was with Ku. He could protect me.

Leticia started in right away, saying, "Oh, it's the pretty little Hmong girl with her cute little boyfriend!"

"Back off, Leticia," I said, and I pushed my quarters into the machine.

Ku just stood there, not saying anything.

"Your friend Frankie isn't here to protect you today, is she? Are you going to have your little ol' boyfriend beat me up?"

I blushed really hard. I wanted to take off, but Ku hadn't got his drink yet.

"Just leave her alone, okay?" Ku said. "What's your problem anyway?"

Then she got all mean-looking and said, "You want to get into it, Hmong boy? I could kick your ass!" She started dancing around him, pretending to fight.

I wanted Ku to hit her in the face. I wanted him to protect me.

"I'm not going to hit a girl," he said. Then he took my hand and said, "Come on, Choua. Let's go get lunch."

I was so relieved it was over that for a second I didn't notice that we were holding hands. Oh my God! It was amazing. I forgot Leticia, and felt my whole body go tingly. Actually, I suddenly felt pretty good about Leticia. Ku was holding my hand *because* we ran into her.

"I love you, Leticia," I said to myself.

We got our trays and our hands slipped apart. I swear, I'll never forget that feeling as long as I live.

We sat down to eat lunch and I told Ku about my problems with Leticia and how Frankie saved me, and I told him about Mai, too. I was surprised at how easy it was to talk to him. He was a good listener, and he asked me questions. He wanted to know about my sister and why she ran away, stuff like that. It was awesome!

It's time to go to bed now. I'm so tired I can hardly keep my eyes open. I really hate Leticia, but I sure am glad I ran into her today.

Wednesday, January 24

Today we went to the International Club meeting. It's going to be every Wednesday at lunchtime. I was kind of sad because it meant not seeing Ku, but I know it's important to keep up with your girlfriends. I notice a lot of girls lose their friends when they start going out with guys. I'm not going to let that happen.

The meeting was in the school music room, and when we walked in there were about thirty kids crowded into the room, mostly girls. There were lots of Asians, some white kids and then I noticed about three black kids, too. They were Leticia's friends! I wanted to get the hell out of that room as quickly as I could. I wasn't going to belong to any club that had those kids in it.

"Come on, let's go," I said, as we stood in the doorway.

"What are you talking about? We just got here!" Frankie said.

"But look who's over there," I whispered, nodding to the back of the room.

"We can't let those girls scare us!" Frankie said, and she took my arm and steered me to some empty seats. Bee and Trisha followed.

A pretty teacher named Miss Farmer was leading the meeting. She's white and she teaches biology, I think. She told us that the club was to help us see that we could all be friends even though we were from different cultures. She said we're going to do different things like have picnics, and clean up garbage and go on hikes and stuff. On Wednesdays we'll just eat lunch together and talk and play games. She had us all go around the room and introduce ourselves.

I think most of us felt kind of shy and we stuck with our own groups, but then Miss Farmer explained a game we were going to play. We each got a list of questions that said things like, "Find someone who has lived in another country" and "Find a person who speaks a language other than English" and "Find someone who lives in your neighborhood." There were about ten questions like that and we had to run around and ask people these questions. When you found someone, they had to sign their name.

I felt nervous, and I *really* didn't want to talk to Leticia's friends. I had to keep telling myself, "It's the new me. I'm going to do what I want and I'm not going to be afraid of stuff."

So I got up like everyone else, took a deep breath, and started walking around the room, asking questions.

I went over to a white girl with blond hair and braces and asked, "Have you ever traveled to a foreign country?"

"Well, I've been to Canada," she said. "Does that count?"

I shrugged my shoulders and said, "Sure. It's not the US."

She signed her name and said, "Do you speak another language?"

I laughed and so did she. She knew I spoke Hmong. I signed my name and I noticed her name was Jennifer. She seemed nice.

I got a bunch of signatures and talked to some new people. It was actually kind of fun. Then one of Leticia's friends came over to me. She said, "I think we live in the same neighborhood. Will you sign for me?"

"Sure," I said, and signed my name. As I was walking away she called my name.

"What?" I asked, turning around.

"I'm sorry about Leticia," she said. "She's not really our friend. She follows us around all the time and we can't seem to get rid of her. We feel kind of sorry for her because she doesn't have any friends."

I think they probably hang out with her because they're scared not to. Even so, it was nice of her to say that to me.

"I wish she'd get off my back," I said. "I've never done anything to her." I didn't feel comfortable talking to this girl, but she seemed to want to keep talking to me.

"You know," she said, "some of us black kids think the Hmong kids hate us and we don't get it. I think that's why Leticia's so nasty. I mean, Hmong kids never talk to us. They stay as far away from us as possible."

I didn't know what to say. I was surprised to hear her say that. I never knew the black kids even thought about us Hmong kids.

I decided to be honest and said, "I think us Hmong are a little scared of black kids. We're pretty quiet and stuff, and black kids..."

I didn't know how to finish my sentence. I was going to say "are always getting into trouble and mouthing off to their teachers," but that didn't seem very nice.

"I know what you mean," she said. "Hmong kids and black kids are pretty different."

Then she smiled and said, "But that's why we're here, right? We're trying to figure out how we're the same so we can be friends."

I wasn't so sure, but I shrugged my shoulders and said, "I guess so."

Just then Miss Farmer told us to come back to our seats again. I'm not sure how I feel about the whole thing. It was nice that she talked to me and all, but I'm just not sure that being friends with black kids is going to work. We'll see.

Saturday, January 27

Well, it's Saturday, and I went to the hospital today to see Ger. I took the bus because I didn't want Mom and Dad to be there. He was moved to a new area last week called the rehab unit which means he's getting a lot better. I wasn't sure when the visiting hours were, but I took a chance and went in the early afternoon. I didn't think they would turn me away.

I wasn't as nervous as last time, but the place still scared me. I bet there are a lot of ghosts in hospitals. I mean, so many people die there. I know not everyone believes in ghosts, but most Hmong do. There were a lot of ghosts in Laos and Thailand. One time last summer my mom wouldn't let us go outside the whole day because she said she saw ghosts waiting outside the house for us. Oh yeah, and there's a teenage ghost that lives in the women's restroom at the Hmong funeral home on Dale Street. She was killed a few years ago, and now she hangs out there. I've never been there, but all the Hmong girls at school talk about it. They're too scared to go to the toilet.

But I made myself not think about ghosts and scary stuff. I needed to think about what I was going to say to Ger instead. I kind of hoped he would be up and walking around, but I knew I was dreaming. He was still in bed, only this time he was sitting up.

"Hi, Ger," I said, trying to sound cheerful. "How's it going?"

"How do you think it's going?" he asked miserably. "I just want to get the hell out of here!"

"Congratulations," I said, trying to change his mood a bit. "I hear you're going to walk. That's so great!"

Ger looked like he wanted to kill me. I didn't understand.

"Come here and look at this," he said.

I walked over to the bed and saw his foot sticking out of the covers. His big toe wiggled.

"That's all I can do. Wiggle my toes. Can I walk? In my dreams!"

I saw that his recovery might not happen as quickly as I thought. I couldn't imagine not being able to walk around or even cross my legs. It must be horrible.

"When do you think you're going to walk again?" I asked.

Ger looked like he hated me.

Oops, I screwed up again. I should never have asked that question. What was I thinking? Did I expect him to jump out of bed and do karate? How stupid can I get!

"You don't get it, do you?" he said angrily. "Maybe I'll be able to walk again. *Maybe*. I can hardly wiggle my toes right now. I wish that bullet had just killed me. It's better than this."

Ger's face was red, and it looked like he might cry again. I felt terrible. I went to the hospital to tell him that he wouldn't be my brother anymore unless he got out of the gang, and here he was, stuck in a hospital bed, not even able to move. I was such a jerk!

"Listen, Ger," I said, sitting down beside the chair beside the bed. "I'm really sorry. This must be just awful. I suck. Sorry for trying to be all cheerful."

"That's okay. What do *you* know?" he said, giving me a half-smile. "You're just a kid."

I hate it when he says that. I'm not just a kid. And I know a lot. He makes it sound like nothing has ever happened to me, like I don't have any feelings. But I didn't want to say anything else to upset him so I just said, "Yeah, you're right."

"Did you hear about my homeboys?" he asked, after a minute.

I nodded my head.

"I can't believe it. All my friends are dead or in jail."

I tried to imagine what that would be like if it happened to my friends. I couldn't. It would be too terrible.

"Are you going to get out of the gang now?" I asked him.

"What gang?" he said angrily. "I just said they're all either dead or in jail. Yeah, Choua, I'm out of the gang. Are you happy now?"

I sat there miserably with my head down. After a while I asked him if there was anything I could get him.

"I just want to be alone," he said. "Thanks for stopping by."

I wish I had never gone.

Tuesday, January 30

I'm writing this in the bathroom because I don't want to go into the bedroom. Mai is in lying on the floor, curled up and sobbing. Dad is outside putting bars on our bedroom window.

It started like this: Mai was playing some rap music really loudly in our bedroom. It didn't bother me because I can do my homework through any kind of noise. Plus, I kind of like rap music. Anyway, Dad yelled at her to turn the music off and she didn't. She turned it up instead. I don't know why she's so stupid. I mean, she could have just turned it down and listened to it quietly and he never would have known.

A few seconds later, I heard Dad yelling outside our door. We like to keep our door locked so my little brothers and sister don't break in and mess everything up and bother us. He was screaming, "Open up the door!" I was too scared to move. I was sitting on my bed, reading a book, and I just stayed there, frozen.

There was a loud noise and the door crashed open. Dad kicked a big hole in it, and he was in the room, looking like a monster. He hardly ever comes into our room so at first he couldn't find the boom box. He spotted it on the desk, yanked the *2 Pac* tape out of it and threw it against the wall.

Then he went for Mai. She was standing beside the closet trying to look brave, but I could tell she was freaking out. He grabbed her by the hair, and pushed her against the wall. Then he grabbed a ruler sitting on the desk and started hitting her. It was horrible to watch. I've never seen Dad so angry. He hit her on the arms and the stomach and the face. In the middle of all the whirling arms and struggling, he yelled, "You're no better than a dog. You're a dog, not my daughter. How dare you disobey me again?"

Mai was screaming and crying, but he just kept hitting her. Ka and Nou ran out of the room, but I couldn't move. It must have gone on for two minutes at least.

At last he stopped and Mai slumped onto the floor. I think he hurt her pretty bad. On his way out of the room he threw the boom box onto the floor and stepped on it really hard. I could hear it crack and break.

I heard him tell my Mom that he was going to the hardware store to buy a new lock for the door and some bars for the window. He's planning to lock us in. He's out there right now putting steel bars on the window—the kind people buy so burglars can't break in. Only these are so we can't break out! Mom is in the kitchen crying. She tried to tell him it was a bad idea, but he yelled at her and told her to shut up, that he knew what was best.

I have to go now and help Mai clean up. She's still crying in the bedroom, all bloody and bruised. She'd better not go to school for a while or some teacher will send a policeman out here to arrest Dad. In Laos, it's okay for parents to beat on their kids if they do something wrong, but you can't do it in America. Once Ka went to school with a black eye and they sent a social worker to our house to make sure my parents hadn't been beating her. She just got it from falling off a swing, but some snoopy teacher had to go and stick her nose into our family business. That's what I hate about this country: they don't respect your culture. If you don't do it their way, you're bad.

I know what my dad did was bad, but he doesn't know how else to control Mai. I think he's really, really scared about what's happening to his kids, and he just doesn't know what to do. I wish he hadn't beat her up, though. And I really don't want my bedroom to turn into a jail, either! Right now I feel sorry for everyone: my dad and Mai and Ger. But you know what? I also feel mad at them all! What's the matter with this family anyway?

Thursday, February 1

The day started off pretty good. Ku and I talked for a few minutes before school, and we sat next to each other in social studies class, and kept smiling at each other. We haven't held hands again, but I keep remembering how good that felt. I really want him to kiss me, but I'm trying to not even think about that. The dance is in two weeks, and I'm really nervous. I can't tell my parents about it, but I need to get a dress somehow. I don't have any money so I haven't figured out how I'm going to do it. I hope my buddies can help me out.

Sunday, February 4

Life has been terrible since Dad put the bars on the window and the lock on the door. It's pretty stupid because he locks the door at bedtime, but one of us always has to get up and go to the bathroom or something. Then we have to pound on the wall between our bedroom and my mom and dad's room. One of them has to get out of bed and let us out. I've heard about some Hmong girls who get chained to their beds so they can't get away. That's awful, but at least if Dad chained Mai to her bed, we wouldn't have to suffer too! I'm pretty angry that I'm being punished for something I didn't do. So is Ka.

At first I felt sorry for Mai after Dad beat her up. She wouldn't let me help her get cleaned up that night even though she was all bloody and messed up. She just sat huddled up in the corner of the room like a caged animal. I didn't know who to be more afraid of—her or Dad.

Now I feel like she deserves what she got. She should know better—she's in so much trouble already. I don't even talk to her these days, but I did do one nice thing for her: I let her borrow my Walkman so she can listen to her music at night and Dad won't hear her. I didn't really give it to her to be nice. Mostly, I don't want to hear her bitch all the time. As long as she's got her music going, she usually shuts up. I don't know how she's going to graduate. As soon as she gets home, she goes straight to the room, turns on her music and lies on the bed. I never see her reading or studying.

Anyway, I've got troubles of my own. The dance is next week, and I have to figure out what I'm going to wear and how to get out of the house. I asked Mom if I could go to Trisha's house for night and she said no because Dad doesn't want us going over to our friends' houses anymore.

"That's so unfair!" I wailed. "Just because Mai and Ger screw up, why should I get punished?"

My mom looked at me sadly and said, "You to be careful, Choua.

If not careful, you be like Mai!"

"I'll never be like Mai!" I yelled at my Mom. "I would never be that stupid!"

I went to the room and slammed the door. I threw myself down on the bed and started to cry. At first I was really angry. I just thought about what a stupid family I had and how I hated being Hmong. Then I decided I would just have to find a way to sneak out. The more I planned it, the more scared I got.

Oh my God, I *am* becoming just like Mai.

Wednesday, February 7

I know my mom is on my side and if only we could sit down and talk, maybe she would understand that I have to go to the dance. I really, really don't want to be like Mai. I don't want to sneak around to get what I want. I want to get what I want by being honest. I have to keep reminding myself that I'm the new me now. The problem is, I keep going back to the old one. But practice makes perfect so I'll keep trying.

This evening I asked my Mom if we could talk. She said she was tired, but I told her it was important. We sat at the kitchen table still filled with dirty dishes from supper.

"Mom," I started by saying, "I want to tell you that I'm not going to be like Mai. I don't want you to worry. I'm not going to get into a gang or anything like that."

She looked at me with a worried look in her eyes, but she didn't say anything.

"I mean it Mom," I said. "Look at me! I work really hard and my grades are good. I have nice friends and we stay out of trouble."

That was sort of a lie, and I felt myself blushing a little as I said it. I thought about smoking pot with Trisha and about going around with Ku. I wanted to tell her about him, but I knew I couldn't. I want to be honest with my Mom, but I know I can't tell her everything. She just wouldn't understand. She's trying, but she's still so Hmong. Plus, she can't go against my dad.

My mom patted me on the knee and said, "You good girl, Choua," she said. "I know you good."

I smiled at her and said, "Mom, it's hard for me because I feel like you and Dad are punishing me because of Ger and Mai's bad behavior. I don't want to be locked in the room and never be allowed to go anywhere. I don't think it's fair. Please let me prove to you that I won't get into trouble."

I still hadn't decided if I was going to tell her about the dance. At first, I thought I might tell her I was just going with my girlfriends, and it would be fine, but she knows that there's lots of dancing and boy/girl contact. The more I thought about it, the more I thought I had better leave that out.

So I said, "Mom, I really want to go to Trisha's house for night next Friday. We planned it for a long time. We're just going to hang out and watch videos and stuff, I promise!"

When I was telling that to my mom, I almost believed it. I hadn't planned to lie to her. But what choice did I have? I have to go to the Valentines dance! Ku and I only see each other once in a while, and I can't wait to dance with him, hold his hand, maybe kiss him? I *had* to lie!

My Mom sighed and said, "I talk to your dad, Choua. I tell him you good girl, okay?"

I gave her a big hug, even though we hardly ever hug. "*Kuv hlub koj niam,*" I said to her which means, "I love you."

My Mom blushed. In Hmong culture, we hardly ever tell our parents that we love them. I could tell she was happy.

So I'm back in my room. I've got to finish my homework and try to push away my feelings of guilt about lying to my mom. But more than feeling guilty, I feel excited. Yippee! I'm going to the dance! I just have to figure out what I'm going to wear.

Friday, February 9

I feel kind of guilty because I haven't been writing about Ger much. I feel even guiltier because I haven't been going to see him. I just felt like such a loser the last time I went, and I'm sure he doesn't want to see me. I've decided to hide him away in a corner of my mind for now so I can concentrate on getting on with *my* life. It's so easy to let my family's problems take over, but I won't let them! *I* don't have problems. I have great friends, I like school, and I have a boyfriend! (Well, kind of.)

Trisha, Frankie, Bee and I are all going to the Valentines dance next week. Bee told her parents she was staying over at Trisha's, and Frankie's family doesn't mind if she goes. I can't wait! A real live date and then a pajama party! It's going to be the best night of my life.

We decided to walk home after school today instead of taking the bus since the weather been really warm for February. It's a pretty long walk from Como to our houses, especially since we walked around part of the lake first where all the rich people live. After you cross the railway tracks the houses are still nice, but a little shabbier. By the time you get to our neighborhood, it's hard to imagine that those mansions along the lake even exist. Frogtown is like a whole different planet.

I got a blister from clumping along in Mai's platforms that I stole from her closet this morning. I know it's stupid to wear shoes like that in the winter. I had to keep holding onto Frankie so I wouldn't slip.

"I don't know what I'm going to wear!" Bee moaned as we were walking. "I don't have any dresses except for my Hmong clothes."

"You'd look like a real geek going to the dance dressed in your traditional clothes!" I laughed. But I've got the same problem. I have no idea what to wear. All I've got are jeans and tee shirts. That would look pretty stupid too!

Frankie's Mom is going to sew her a new dress for the prom.

Trisha's mom has a friend who owns a dress store so she's going to get her outfit from there.

"I have an idea," Trisha said. "My mom has a closet full of pretty dresses. She's not much taller than you two. Let's go try some on and see if they fit!"

It's true that Trisha's mom is not very tall, but she's pretty sexy. She's got a great figure. I didn't think any of her clothes could fit me.

"I guess we could give it a try," I said, so we all ended up at Trisha's house trying on her mother's clothes and makeup. She had a lot of pretty dresses, but none of them looked right on Bee or myself. We looked like we were playing dress-up.

I was ready to give up and just phone Ku and tell him I couldn't go when Trisha said, "Hey! I just remembered something. My sister used to go to the prom every year in high school. I wonder if any of her old dresses are still around here."

She raced to the storage area in the basement, went through a few boxes, and sure enough, she pulled out three or four dresses that were definitely from old dances. They looked a little frilly and shiny for me, but it was my last hope.

Bee and I stripped down and slipped into the dresses. I took the plainest one I could fine—a pale yellow silky dress that had no sleeves. It had a big bow in the back and a frill on the bottom, but otherwise it wasn't too geeky. Bee took a very shiny, ruffled pink one that I wouldn't be caught dead in, but once she got it zipped up, she actually looked pretty good. Bee is just a little bit chubby, and this dress made her look really pretty and slim. She twirled around and danced across the room.

"Maybe this dress will help me meet the boy of my dreams," she said. Then she kissed the mirror, real sexy-like, like it was a boy.

"Come on, Choua, try yours on," Frankie said.

I slipped it on over my bra and panties, and looked into the mirror. It was kind of big, and it made me look like I had no chest at all. The big bow in the back made me look like a Christmas present.

I sighed deeply. "I guess I just won't be going to the dance," I said.

"Oh come on," Trisha said, "It's not that bad. You could wear a shawl and..."

Frankie interrupted Trisha. "Hey! My mom can help you!" she said, "She's really good at fixing dresses. She was a tailor in Liberia. You come to my house and she'll turn it into a Cinderella dress!"

Well, it's worth a try, I guess. So tomorrow, I'm going to bring the dress over to Frankie's house and we'll see what happens.

We practiced putting up our hair and putting on makeup until it was time to race home for supper. I didn't want to worry my mom or make her not trust me. I carefully washed off all the makeup before I left, and I stuffed the yellow dress into my backpack. When I got home, my Mom was just setting the table for dinner.

"Let me help you with that," I said, taking the plates from her hands. "Sorry I'm late. I had to go to the library after school. I have a big research project I'm working on and I have to get an A."

I've become so good at lying that the words just spill out without me even thinking about it anymore.

Friday, February 16

I told Ku I'd meet him at school the evening of the dance. He knows that most Hmong parents don't let their daughters go to dances, especially if they have a date with a boy. Frankie's mom ended up fixing the dress real nice. She made it tighter around the boobs, and took the ruffle off the bottom and the bow in the back. It looks very simple, but elegant. I borrowed a colorful silk shawl from Trisha's mom to wear over the dress in case I got cold.

We all rushed over to Trisha's house to get ready after school. Her mom is so cool. She told her boss at the restaurant she was coming to work late so she could help us all get ready. I just pray my parents don't call here. I don't think that's going to happen, though. I don't think they even know Trisha's last name.

First we did each other's hair. Frankie's was already braided into hundreds of tiny braids, but we put it up in a big bun on top of her head and let a few of the braids hang loose. Then we worked on Bee's hair. It's pretty short so we couldn't put it up. We poufed it up and sprayed it, and put a bit of glitter in it. Trisha was next. She wanted hers down and curly so we helped her mom put hot rollers in her hair. Boy, did she look glamorous! Her curls just tumbled all over her shoulders. We decided I would go last since I was the most important. Just for tonight, that is, because I have a date and none of the others do. They're all going together as a threesome. I'm sure they'll follow me around all night anyway.

Right now the girls are doing each other's makeup. My hair is up in a French roll with little wisps of hair hanging down, but I'm still wearing my jeans and tee shirt and I don't have any makeup on yet. They're saving me for last again.

Ms. Martinez taught me to carry my notebook with me wherever I go so I can always write when I have a chance or when I get a great idea. It just felt like the right moment to sneak away and have some private time to write a bit.

Actually, I'm really nervous about tonight. What if Ku doesn't like me as much as I thought he did? What if I look ugly and he doesn't want to be seen with me? What if my parents find out I've been at the dance? I've got butterflies in my stomach from being nervous and feeling guilty.

Mai lent me a little purse to carry with me. We were lying in bed last night and I was so excited that I couldn't keep the secret to myself. When I told them, Ka and Mai were both really excited for me, and they promised they wouldn't breathe a word to Mom and Dad. Mai got out of bed, turned on the lights and started ripping apart the closet. She gave me this pretty little purse to use and some mints to keep my breath fresh.

"He might want to kiss you," she said. I got all red, but I didn't say anything. I hope so.

She also gave me some light pink lipstick she said would look really pretty with my dress. I thought that was very nice of her. I don't know if she's excited for me or she's just proud that I'm being a bad girl, like her. Anyway, I'm not so mad at her right now.

Well, I have to go. Trisha and the girls are ready to do my face. This could be the greatest night of my life. I feel a little like Cinderella.

~~~

Trisha's mom dropped us off at school just before seven o'clock. It's a good thing she has a car. We would have looked pretty stupid wearing our fancy dresses on the bus! I was feeling kind of pretty for the first time in my life. I carried the little purse Mai gave me with the mints, the lipstick, some mascara and some Kleenex. Trisha's mother told us we should go to the bathroom once in a while to check our makeup because it could start to run if we got too sweaty from the dancing and hot lights.

I didn't want it to look like we were all waiting for Ku because it might make him nervous so the others went in ahead of me while I waited at the gym entrance. We had agreed to meet at seven o'clock. By five after seven, I was starting to get nervous. By ten after seven, I thought I was going to die. I couldn't believe he wasn't there! Had he stood me up?

I felt my eyes welling up with tears, and I tried to choke them back. I was scared the mascara would run and make me look like a raccoon. I wanted to go hide in a restroom stall and cry and cry. But suddenly there he was.

"Boo," he said. "Sorry, I'm late. My stupid brother was supposed to drop me off, but he completely forgot and went out with his friends instead of coming home. I had to get a ride from my cousin."

So he hadn't stood me up! I gave him a big smile and said, "That's okay. I knew you would come."

Some of the boys had given the girls flowers to pin on their dresses. I think they're called corsages. It didn't look like Ku had anything for me, but that was okay since lots of Hmong boys don't know about stuff like that. But suddenly, he pulled a single red rose from behind his back.

"Surprise," he said.

How romantic! I loved it, but I didn't know what to do with it. I held onto it for a while, and then I ended up shoving it in my purse where it got squished. I'll keep the petals forever, though. They'll remind me of my first date.

We went into the dark gym. There were mirrored balls hanging from the ceiling spinning around. There were all kinds of kids, most

of them dressed up fancy. Ku was only dressed up a little. He had on a pair of khaki pants and a button down shirt with a tie. Some of the white boys were wearing tuxedos, but I thought they looked like geeks. Ku looked gorgeous.

"Hey," he said, all of a sudden. "I didn't tell you how great you look."

I blushed really red, and said, "No, I don't. I look like I'm playing dress-up."

I shouldn't have said that. Ms. Martinez once told me you should always accept compliments that are given to you. She said you should always smile and say thank-you.

"No, really," Ku said. "You look beautiful."

I didn't know what to say, but then he said, "Hey, want to dance?"

So we went out on the dance floor and I suddenly remembered that I had no idea how to dance. I was pretty embarrassed, but Ku was great. He was hopping all over the place like a jackrabbit, and I kind of just stood in one place and swayed back and forth. I must have looked like an idiot.

After a few more songs, Ku asked, "Is it okay if I go and talk to my friends for a while? I'll come find you in a bit."

"Sure," I said, but I felt disappointed. There hadn't even been a slow song yet, and I thought this was *our* night together. I went off to find my friends. They were standing by the punch bowl looking like they were having a great time, laughing with some of the other girls from the International Club.

"Hey, here comes Choua," Bee announced. "Where's your hot date?"

I shrugged my shoulders. "He went to talk to his friends." Then I started to cry. I didn't mean to. It just happened.

The girls all crowded around me. "What's the matter?" everyone was asking, and I just felt so embarrassed. I kept thinking my face must be striped like a zebra from all the mascara dripping from my eyes. The evening had just begun and I was crying already.

We went to the bathroom and Trisha got me cleaned up while I told them everything was okay, it just wasn't perfect like I had expected.

"The evening's just started, Choua," Frankie said. "Give it some time."

"I know, I know," I said. "I can't believe I'm being so stupid."

After a while we went back out into the gym and all danced together and drank punch. It must have been half an hour before Ku came over and found me.

"Hi," he said to everyone shyly. And then he said, "Can I talk to you, Choua?"

My heart started to race. Why did he want to talk to me? Was he going to break up with me?

"Okay," I said and walked away from my friends, wishing they could come with me.

He said, "Let's go outside."

The rule at school dances is once you leave the school, you're not allowed back in because they think kids might sneak in drugs and alcohol. The principal and a policeman and lots of teachers were hanging out by the doors.

"What happens if we want to go back in?" I asked. I didn't want to leave my friends behind.

"Don't worry. I've got a cell phone," he said. "I'll give Seng a call when we're ready to come in again. He'll meet us at the far door."

We walked out of the gym and into the parking lot. It was cold, and I felt like I was ready to cry again. It was dark and the stars were shining. The moon was just a tiny fingernail.

"I've got the key's to Seng's car. We can go sit in there and warm up," he said. We walked over to the red Honda Civic, and Ku opened my side for me before getting in the driver's seat. Nobody has ever opened a door for me. He turned on the engine to get the car warmed up. We were quiet for a while, but then I couldn't stand it any longer.

"What did you want to talk to me about?" I asked him. "Are you going to tell me that you want to break up with me?"

Then I started to cry again! I can't believe what a crybaby I am. We just sat there with the car engine running, me blowing my nose, sobbing, chattering my teeth, and Ku just staring at me.

"Oh God," I kept thinking, "He must just hate me."

When I had finally calmed down a bit, he said, "Choua, I just asked you out here because I wanted to kiss you. I don't want to break up with you. I've been dying to kiss you, and I don't think I can wait any longer."

Then he leaned over the gears, put his arms on my shoulders, and gave me this perfect kiss. It was long and kind of wet and just.... I don't even feel like I can describe it. It was perfect. I wasn't sure I would know what to do when someone kissed me for the first time, but it wasn't that hard. Once you're kissing, you're don't even think. You're so caught up in the moment, you just do it.

We sat there for a long time, our arms wrapped around each

other. I was really warm, and my teeth weren't chattering anymore. I noticed some other cars running. We weren't the only ones making out. I felt so happy and excited, and every part of my body was tingling. I think we were both kind of embarrassed and neither of us knew what to say. But what did we need to say? We just started kissing some more.

We kissed for most of the night. It was kind of uncomfortable kissing over the gear shift, and my dress kept slipping off my shoulders. I was all twisted up and uncomfortable, but I didn't care. The stars were shining and we put on a *Snoop Doggy Dogg* tape that was in the glove compartment. Why dance when you could kiss? I never knew anything could feel so good. It was pretty much the most awesome feeling I've ever had. I also want to say that Ku was a real gentleman. He didn't try anything else. Even though I kind of wanted him to, I'm glad he didn't. I wonder if he's ever kissed a girl before. He seemed to know what he was doing. I don't even want to think about that. I'm the only woman for Ku.

Right now I'm sitting in Trisha's bathroom writing this all down while the girls are pigging out on chips and ice cream in the next room and watching videos. I want to get it all written down so I never forget it as long as I live.

At ten-thirty I saw Trisha's mom pulling into the parking lot.

"Ku, I have to go," I said. "My ride is here."

"Tonight was the bomb," he said. "Can I see you this weekend?"

This weekend? I didn't know how I would do it, but I said, "Yeah, I'll call you tomorrow, okay. What's your number?"

He quickly wrote it down on a scrap of paper on the floor and a pen he found in the back seat. We snuck back to the gym entrance to wait for the others. He touched my arm and said, "Let me kiss you one more time, Choua." So we had one last, long kiss that I can still taste.

When the girls saw me, they gave me a funny look.

"What?" I said.

"What happened to your lips?" Bee asked.

"What are you talking about?"

"They've got a big rash all around them, like you were in poison ivy or something!" Frankie said.

Then they all laughed, and Trisha said, "Well, no wonder we couldn't find Choua all night. She was out necking with her boyfriend Ku!"

We didn't say anything all the way home, but as soon as we got to Trisha's room they made me tell them absolutely everything. I went straight to the mirror to look at myself. it was true! My lips are all rashy like a baby's butt! They'd better be cleared up by the time I go home tomorrow or I'm going to be in BIG trouble!

Saturday, February 17

I went home after breakfast this morning. My lips looked a lot better, and I didn't think anybody would be able to tell I had been kissing unless they looked real close. I couldn't wait to call Ku, but I didn't want to seem too anxious so I decided to wait until after lunch. I knew I wouldn't be able to go out at night again, so I hoped he would be able to meet me in the afternoon. I thought I could tell my mom I was going to the library or something like that. She likes it when I go to the library so that's my best excuse.

As soon as I got in the house, Ka and Mai cornered me in the bedroom and made me tell them everything. At first I didn't want to say anything, but then Mai looked at me real hard, and said, "Look Ka, she's been kissing!"

"I have not," I lied.

"Don't try to lie to me, little Sister," Mai said. "Anybody with experience knows that you've been kissing. Let me see your neck," she said, grabbing my tee shirt and yanking it down.

"Hey, cut that out!" I said angrily. "Just because I kissed a boy doesn't mean I have hickeys all over my body. I'm not like you, Mai!"

"Okay, okay," Mai said. "You say you're not like me, but I don't believe you. First you lie to Mom and Dad about where you're going, and then you end up kissing some boy all night. That sounds a lot like me!"

I started unpacking my backpack, not answering. I don't want to think about it. All I want to do is be with Ku. Just because I have a crush on a boy and we kissed a little bit, it doesn't mean I'm like Mai!

I helped clean up around the house, but all I could think about was calling him. At noon I called him, but I didn't need to look at the slip of paper with his number on it because I'd already memorized it.

A woman, probably his mother, answered the phone. I suddenly felt really embarrassed. I asked for him in Hmong. "*Kub pus nyob tsev os?*"

"Just a minute," she said, and I heard her calling him.

He came to the phone, and I didn't know what to say.

"It's me," I said.

"I know. I've been waiting," he answered.

"So, what's up?" I asked.

There was a pause.

"It's hard for me to talk right now, Choua. Where can we meet?"

"How about the library?" I said. "That's where I usually meet my friends. My mom doesn't mind when I go there."

"The Lexington Library?" he asked.

"Yeah. How about one-thirty?"

"Sounds good. I'll see you then."

And that was it. I hung up the phone, and I was shaking all over. I didn't know what was going to happen next. All I wanted to do in the whole world was to be with Ku.

I got changed, put some books in my bag, told my mom I was going to the library and that I'd be home before dinner. She just nodded her head, and kept chopping the chicken.

"Thank God," I thought. "That was easy."

When I got to the library, Ku was already there. As soon as I saw him, I blushed. He looked kind of shy too.

"Where do you want to go?" he asked.

"Aren't we going to study?" I said.

He looked sad and confused. It made me laugh. "Just kidding, silly."

We couldn't really think of any place to go around University Avenue, but Ku had his bicycle, and he suggested we go to Como Park. There are lots of private places there. So I climbed on his bar and he pedaled for a while, but we ended up walking most of the way because the bar really hurt my skinny butt. We found an area that had a lot of trees, close to where I had gone with Trisha and Ken.

"How's this?" he asked.

"Good," I said, smiling at him shyly.

We sat down against a tree and started kissing. The ground was wet, but we didn't care. It was as wonderful as I remembered it. It felt really, really good—better than an ice cream sundae with extra chocolate sauce. But suddenly, I started to feel kind of sick to my stomach. Something wasn't right.

"What's the matter?" Ku asked as I pushed him away.

"I don't know," I answered. "I just don't know if we should be doing this, you know?"

"Why not?" he asked.

"You're Hmong. You know why. If our parents knew, they'd kill us, especially mine."

"Who cares about our parents?" he said angrily. "Just because we're Hmong, it doesn't mean we can't make out! That doesn't make sense. I like you. You like me. What's the matter?"

I couldn't really answer him. My feelings are so mixed up about what's right and what's wrong. Is everything American wrong? Is everything Hmong right? Or is it the other way around? I didn't use to think about it very much, but now it's on my mind a lot.

I answered, "I can't explain it, Ku. Don't you ever feel mixed up about what you should and shouldn't do? I mean, I have a brother and a sister who are both in gangs. Ger is shot, and thanks to Mai, us girls have a lock on our bedroom door and bars on our window. Now I feel like I'm acting just like her!"

I started to cry. He had sure seen me cry a lot for someone who's only been out with me twice. He wiped away the tears from my cheek. I thought that was really sweet.

"Don't cry, Choua," he said. "It makes me so sad when you cry. Hey, you know what?" Then he took my hand and he held it. "If you don't think we should be messing around, let's not."

I looked up at him through my blurry eyes. "Really?" I said. "You'd still want to go out with me even if we didn't fool around?"

Ku breathed deeply and looked down. "I've got to be honest with you, Choua. All I want to do is make out with you. It's all I can think about. It's gonna be really hard for me. You know what I mean?"

I got all red and warm again. I still couldn't figure out how someone like me could turn on a boy like him. I'm nothing special. Even though the only thing in the world I wanted to do was be with him, I knew what I had to do.

"Ku, I feel the same way about you. You're all I can think about, too." I took a deep breath, and I knew what I had to say. It was the hardest thing I've ever said in my almost 16 years on the earth. "That's why I think we'd better not see each other any more. I'm scared of what could happen if we hang out too much."

Ku stared at me, like he couldn't believe what I was saying. "You're kidding, right?" he said. "You just said you wanted me so bad, and now you're breaking up with me? I don't get it!"

I didn't get it either. What was I thinking? One side of me was just wanting to curl up in his arms and stay with him forever, and the other side was saying, "Choua, be careful."

"Ku, I don't get it either," I said. I was so embarrassed that I could hardly spit out what was on my mind. "I just feel like...well...kissing you is so great, and..."

I couldn't finish my sentence. I was too embarrassed to tell him that I was scared we might go all the way. Hmong girls don't talk about sex.

"But if two people really like each other, what's wrong with it?" Ku asked.

"You know what's wrong with it," I said. I got up and picked up my bag. "Maybe it's different for boys, Ku, but if my dad finds out about us, I'll be grounded forever. And you know what else? He'll make sure I get married ASAP! Maybe it's okay for American girls to sleep around, but if we do, our lives are over!"

"But nobody needs to find out," he said.

I made myself think about Youa and Tou and their babies, and how Youa struggled to get through school and lost all her friends. I thought of Mai and Ger and how messed up their lives were.

"I'm sorry, Ku. I've made up my mind. I can't see you any more," I said.

I've never seen anyone look so sad. He picked up his backpack and got on his bike.

"See you around, then," he said as he rode away. He didn't even try to argue. I kind of wish he had.

I've been sitting under this tree shivering and crying my eyes out for the last two hours. I think I did the right thing, but why does it have to hurt so much? Did I make a mistake? I couldn't wait to become a teenager in elementary school. I thought it would be so much fun. Life would be exciting and you could do whatever you wanted. Right now I wish I was in first grade again, learning how to read. I think that was the happiest time of my life.

You know what? As soon as I try *not* to be like Mai, everything gets messed up. What am I supposed to do—join a gang? Maybe Mai is right about gangs. Anything is better than my life right now. I have to walk home now and pretend nothing ever happened. I don't know what else to do.

~~~

When I got home, Dad was waiting for me. He said my little brother Pao had spotted me with some boy on a bike riding down Lexington Parkway. He grabbed me and shook me hard, bruising my arm.

"I thought you were a good girl!" he yelled. "How can you do this? First your sister and then Ger and now you. Do you want to kill both of your parents? You're breaking our hearts!"

Just when I thought things couldn't get any worse, they just had. I thought maybe I could tell my dad I had just broken up with Ku, but I knew that would be a waste. He was too angry to listen, and then I would have to tell him about all my other lies too. I expected him to hit me, but he just told me to go to my room, and then he locked the door behind me. So here I am sitting in this jail cell wondering how things could possibly get any worse.

Yesterday I was in love with Ku and I went to bed dreaming of his kisses. Today I decide to do the right thing, and I mess everything up. I'll never be with Ku again, and my parents will never trust me again. I must be dreaming. Real life couldn't be this terrible.

~~~

My mom brought me some supper at about seven o'clock tonight, but she didn't talk to me or even look at me. I feel just awful that I betrayed her. I haven't been out of the room for hours and hours. I've been trying really hard not to think about how crappy my life is. I've done all my homework for the weekend, and I'm reading *Gathering of Days*, about a girl who keeps a journal like I do. But my mind keeps wondering back to Ku. I really want to phone Trisha or Bee or Frankie to talk to them about what happened, but I'll probably never be allowed to talk on the phone again.

When Nou fell asleep, Ka and Mai and I came up with a plan. I don't know if I should do it or not, but I feel like I have no choice. Mai has convinced me to run away with her. Really late tonight Ka is going to pound on the wall and tell Mom and Dad that she has a really bad stomach ache. She's going to take a long time in the bathroom and when my mom isn't looking (she's the one who usually gets up and unlocks the door), Mai and I are going to sneak out of the house and make a run for it. My backpack is ready to go. I have a few clean clothes, this journal, my wallet and my toothbrush. At first, I didn't want to do it, but Mai said that Dad's going to keep me locked up in this room until I graduate or he marries me off, whichever comes first. The more I think about it, the more I believe her. He's never going to trust me again. I didn't mean to, but I really, really messed up. I don't think I'll ever be able to straighten it out no matter how hard I try.

So I guess my new life begins tonight. I have no idea what to expect. I just know I've got to leave. Mai is right after all.

Sunday, February 18

I'm writing this in the basement of Shoua's house. She's one of Mai's friends from the gang. We're hiding out for a few days. Shoua's parents are out of town at some family party so we're safe until they come back. It's okay so far because I've got a warm place to sleep and food to eat. I don't know what's going to happen when we have to leave here though. I'm trying not to think about it.

Mai is upstairs playing loud music with her friends. There are boys over too. We got here in the middle of the night yesterday, and

I've been in the basement ever since except when I go upstairs to get food. There's a bathroom with a shower in the basement so I don't even have to go upstairs for that. I don't want to be with Mai and all her homeboys. I may have run away, but I'm not joining her gang!

The longer I sit down here, the more I wonder if I made a big mistake. Tomorrow is Monday, and I guess I can't go to school or I'll get caught for sure. I have all sorts of questions: What's going to happen to me when I get caught? Have my parents called the police? Do my friends know that I've run away? Man, I think I'm screwed.

Things are getting louder and louder upstairs. I know they're drinking beer and probably making out. The whole thing freaks me out. I keep on thinking about Ms. Martinez and the telephone number that is on that piece of paper in my wallet. I keep pulling it out and looking at it. I really want to call her, but I don't think I should get her involved. This is a big deal, and I don't want to get her into trouble. I don't think this is what she meant when she said I could call her any time.

~ ~ ~

Things started to get scary a few hours ago. I could hear Mai crying, and it sounded like some boys were attacking her. She was saying, "Stop, please stop!" At first, I was too scared to go upstairs. I kept saying to myself, "Don't get involved. It's none of your business. Mai got herself into this mess. Let her get out of it."

Finally, I couldn't stand it any more. I went up the stairs and listened quietly by the door for a second before opening it. It sounded like there were a lot of people, but I could still hear Mai crying. Nobody seemed to be doing anything about it. I peeked in the door that opened into the kitchen. There were a bunch of guys sitting on the floor and the counter drinking beer. Last time I was up to fix a sandwich the kitchen had been kind of clean, but now it looked like a tornado had hit it. There were beer cans everywhere, and garbage all over the floor. It stank like cigarettes and pot.

"Hey, who's that kid?" someone asked when they saw me.

"That's just Mai's kid sister," another guy answered. "They ran away together."

"She's kinda cute," said a boy wearing a red bandanna.

"Shut up and leave her alone. Keep your dirty mitts off of her!" Shoua said, coming into the kitchen. "She's not part of this gang, so don't go screwing around with her."

"Yeah? Who says?" the boy asked.

"I do!" Shoua said. "I mean it!" I've never liked Shoua much, but she seemed all right to me at that moment.

I pushed through the kitchen, looking for Mai. I found her in a dirty bedroom, lying on the floor, rolled up in a blanket. She was alone.

"Mai, are you all right?" I asked. "What's going on?"

Mai was crying softly. "I should never have brought you here," she said. "I'm so sorry, Choua. You've got to get out of here. It's not safe."

"What about you?" I asked. I noticed that her clothes were ripped and her jeans had been pulled off.

"It's too late for me, Choua. I screwed up my life a long time ago. I don't want you to do the same thing."

"It's not too late," I said. "Come on, Mai. Just get dressed and we'll get out of here together. Come on!"

"You don't understand, Choua," she said. "I can't go. If I left, they'd come find me again. Besides, these are my homeboys. They take care of me. I don't have anywhere else to go. But if you tell Mom and Dad that I made you run away with me, they might still forgive you. You can work it out with them."

I wasn't thinking about myself for the first time in a long, long time. I was really worried about Mai. She seemed like a tiny little helpless girl, and I felt like I needed to help her.

"I know what I have to do, Mai," I said. "Don't worry about me. But I'm worried about you. Did you get raped? Are you okay?"

"I'm fine," she said, sitting up and brushing away her tears. "It's no big deal. It's just what happens. You get used to it. I have a reputation, Choua. I'm the bad girl. The guys like that. They want to screw me and I let them."

"You don't have to let them!" I said. "Besides, I heard you telling them to stop and they didn't. That's rape! You can't call these guys your friends when they rape you. Are you crazy?"

I felt mad at her and sorry for her all at once. I don't know which emotion was stronger. I felt mad because she was letting people walk all over her. She had given up. I felt sorry for her because I think maybe it's too late for her, just like she said. She's so deep into trouble I don't know if there's any way she can climb out of the hole.

"Choua, do me a favor and just get out of here, okay?" Mai said weakly. "I know you don't understand."

I really felt like the big sister. I looked at her helplessly and had no idea what to do. She grabbed my arm and said, "Choua, I know I screwed up. I know that I've probably ruined my life by joining a gang."

"But it's not too late," I interrupted.

"Just shut up and listen to me," she said. "You can learn from my mistakes. You see what it's like. Go back to Mom and Dad and find a way to work it out. Just promise me you'll never join a gang."

She grabbed my arm harder. "Promise me!" she demanded.

Watching her lying there, half-dressed, tears rolling down her face, her body bruised, I was never so sure of anything in my life. I had already promised Youa, Ger and my mom. Now it was time for my last promise.

"I promise, Mai." And I meant it.

~~~

I begged Mai to let me help her, but she wouldn't. She just told me to leave and make things right. She also asked me to tell my parents that she was sorry.

I went down to the basement and locked the door behind me. I shoved everything into my backpack, and got out of there as fast as I could. I knew it was just a matter of time before those boys came after me, and I wasn't going to let that happen. So instead of going upstairs again, I decided to crawl out of a window. I pushed a table up to the window, climbed up on it, and squeezed my body through the tiny window. I landed in some prickly bushes that scratched me up pretty good. Then I ran all the way to the Citgo gas station on Dale Street. I pulled the crumpled paper out of my wallet, put my 35 cents into the pay phone, and punched in the numbers with a shaking hand.

On the third ring, Ms. Martinez answered. "Hello?"

"Ms. Martinez?"

There was a pause.

"Choua, is that you?"

"Yes," was all I could say before I started crying. I felt pretty stupid standing there in the Citgo parking lot, crying like a waterfall.

"Calm down, Sweetie," she said. "Tell me where you are."

I managed to tell her.

"Are you okay? Are you in danger?"

"Not at this second," I said.

"Okay then, don't move. I'll be there in 15 minutes." And she hung up.

I sat on the curb of the parking lot, shaking like crazy even though I was wearing a heavy sweater and my coat. I had no idea what was going to happen. I was just relieved that Ms. Martinez was coming. I knew she would help me make the right choices. I didn't trust myself to know what to do anymore.

That was when I realized that for the first time that sometimes you need to ask for help. "You don't have to do everything all by yourself. It's okay to ask for help," I kept telling myself.

Ms. Martinez showed up pretty fast, but it felt like forever. A few cop cars drove by while I was sitting there. I wanted to run and hide, but I thought that would look suspicious so I just stayed there and took my chances.

Ms. Martinez sped up in her white Toyota, jumped out of the car, and ran over to me. She hugged me for a long time. It felt so good.

"Choua, are you okay?"

I nodded.

"Come on, I'm taking you to my place. We'll talk there."

She drove me to her apartment just off Grand Avenue. It was small and full of carpets and wall hangings that looked Mexican. She had lots of tables and they were filled with different pots and jars and framed pictures of people. In our house the only table we have is the one in the kitchen, and we only use jars to put stuff in, not as decorations. It was very cozy and warm feeling, though it felt awfully full to me. I think maybe she should get herself a bigger place.

First, young lady," she said, "I'm going to run you a nice hot bath and make you some dinner. Then we're going to talk. All right?"

She looked at me and smiled. I smiled back. At that moment that I knew everything was going to be okay.

So here I am in her pajamas, sitting in a big fluffy chair, and drinking cocoa. I got all cleaned up in a nice bubble bath. She has fluffy yellow towels and her bathroom is full of little bottles of perfume and beauty stuff. I sprayed some on my shiny, hot skin and even sprinkled on some baby powder. Then I went into the kitchen and had some mushroom soup and a tuna sandwich. I wish I could live here forever.

Ms. Martinez has been on the phone for the last half hour or so, but now it's time to tell her exactly what happened. Wish me luck.

~~~

After I finished telling Ms. Martinez everything she said, "Choua, I noticed you were writing earlier. I hope you've been writing all this down. This is going to be an amazing book. A lot of kids can learn from you and your story. I've never met someone with such an interesting life!"

We both laughed. I felt like it was the first time I had laughed in years.

"I write everything," I said. "Everywhere I go, every chance I get. It's the only way I can feel better and work out my feelings."

"Wow! You're amazing," she said after I showed her . "Most people don't write this much in their entire lives!" I've already filled up three notebooks. I think I've written more than a hundred pages.

"There's a lot of mistakes with grammar and spelling and stuff," I said.

"Who cares?" she said. "It's the story that counts. I can help you with all that other stuff. You're a writer, Choua. You're a real writer!"

"Well, I've got a lot to write about," I said, and we both laughed again. I felt so proud.

Then she got serious. "Okay Choua," she said, "we've got to figure this out. Let's go through this one step at a time..."

We decided we would call my parents and tell them I was okay, and that I would be spending the night with her. Then she said we had to call the police department and tell them where Mai was. I was a little uncomfortable with that, but I knew it was the best thing. It made sense. I didn't like the idea of turning Mai in, but I was really afraid for her, too. I think she is probably safer in jail than with her homeboys. At least she'll get four square meals a day and a bed to sleep in.

So I let her get on the phone with the police and then with my parents. My mom insisted on talking to me. I was nervous, but Ms. Martinez nodded and gave me an encouraging smile so I took the phone from her. We spoke in Hmong.

"Mom," I said. "I'm okay. I'm so sorry. I'm so sorry."

"Choua," she sobbed. "My little girl. I'm so happy you're okay. I thought you were dead."

I was surprised she wasn't yelling at me. I always knew she loved me, but at that moment, I had never been so sure. It made me feel like there was hope.

"Mom," I said, "I really want to make things right. I know I messed up really bad, but we can work it out. Please give me another chance. I really love you. I'm so sorry I let you down."

My mom was very gentle with me. She said, "You go to sleep now, Choua. Tomorrow we'll see you and talk. We'll find a way to work things out. We don't want to lose you."

"Mom, you'll never lose me," I answered, and I handed the phone back to Ms. M. She talked with my father and they made arrangements to meet tomorrow afternoon at Lao Family Center. I guess Ms. M. had talked to them on the phone while I was writing earlier.

"You did the right thing," she said after hanging up the phone. "I'm so glad you phoned me. It's going to be hard, but I'll help you get through this. You're a brave girl!"

She made up the couch for me to sleep on and told me I should sleep as long as I needed to in the morning.

"It looks like neither one of us will be going to school on Monday morning," she said. "But that's okay. The weekend went too fast anyway. I could use another day off."

She went to bed and I've been sitting here writing ever since. She said not to worry about tomorrow, that she'd take care of the details. I don't know what they are, but I trust her completely. I'm too exhausted to figure anything else out. I'm practically falling asleep with the pen in my hand. I'll talk to you again tomorrow.

Monday, February 19

I didn't wake up until after ten in the morning. I felt like I hadn't slept so good in years. Ms. Martinez made me eggs and bacon and toast and we drank orange juice and tea. I usually only eat a pop tart for breakfast so this was enormous.

"It's going to be a big day," she said. "You have to be strong."

I thought about Mai, who was probably in jail, and about Ger in the hospital, and about my parents and all their worries. I also thought about Ku. All of it made me feel sad, but it also helped me know that I had to be strong.

Ms. Martinez told me we were going to meet a guy named Brian who was a social worker or something at the Lao Family Center on University Avenue. She said he'd talk with me first, and then my mom and dad would join us later and we'd figure out what to do.

"Will you stay with me?" I asked.

"You bet I will," she said. "You can count on me. I'm going to help you get through this, Sweetie."

I love it when she calls me that. Nobody else has ever called me that. It makes me feel so special and loved. Maybe she calls everyone that, but I don't care.

We hung out at her place for a while and then drove down to Lao Family. I've been there before for different Hmong events, but I never knew they helped kids and their families figure out their problems. On the drive there I felt a little nervous, but I felt safer knowing Ms. Martinez was going to stick around. I also felt better remembering my mom's voice yesterday. I know how much she loves me and I'm pretty sure my dad feels the same way, even if he would never say it.

Brian was a really nice Hmong man. He didn't seem very old, maybe just out of college. He asked if I would like to speak in English or Hmong and I said English. I didn't say it just because of Ms. Martinez, either. I think that I speak better English than I do Hmong. I think in English and I dream in English. It's kind of weird. I wonder if that means I'm more American than Hmong.

Brian asked me a lot of questions about what was going on in my life lately, why I ran away, and what it was like at home. It was kind of strange telling everything to a stranger, especially a Hmong man, but he was a good listener. He said, "I understand" a bunch of times while I was talking, and I really believed him. While I talked, he took notes.

When I had finished telling him everything I asked, "What's going to happen to me?"

"I'm going to be honest with you, Choua. I don't want to hide anything from you," he said. "There's some pretty serious stuff going on with you and your family, and we're going to get you and your parents some help working this out."

I nodded. I completely agreed.

Then he said, "I don't think it's best for you to be living at home right now."

"What?" I sucked in my breath, like someone had punched me. "What do you mean? Where would I go?" I looked at Ms. Martinez in a panic, and she took my hand and held it tightly.

"Do you have any older brothers or sisters you could stay with? Maybe some cousins?" he asked. Then he added, "Just until we get things worked out."

I thought about Youa first. I could go live with her. But why couldn't I just go home? I wanted to cuddle up in my mother's arms and let her stroke my hair. She used to do that when I was a little girl sometimes.

"Listen," I said desperately, "couldn't we just talk to my parents and work it all out so I can go home with them? I don't want to leave home!" I felt the tears spilling over my eyes which were still red and puffy from all the crying I've been doing the last few days.

"It's not that easy, Choua," Brian said. "Please don't be upset. We're going to work everything out, but it doesn't happen overnight. It's going to take a while. You're just going to have to be patient."

My parents were waiting outside so I tried to pull myself together. I knew I would have to be strong and show them I was going to get their trust back. I forced myself to push the idea of having to live somewhere else out of my mind so I could concentrate on dealing with my parents.

As if she were reading my mind, Ms. Martinez said, "One step at a time, Choua. Be strong and you'll get through this. Remember, I'm here for you."

My parents knocked and came in. My mom hugged me, but my dad didn't.

Brian introduced himself and Ms. Martinez to my parents, and we all sat down. Before we started, my mom patted Ms. M.'s hand and said, "Thank you so much for take care my daughter. You kind woman. Thank you."

Ms. M. smiled and said, "You have a very special daughter, Mrs. Vang. I care about her very much."

That made me feel ready to be strong. We switched to talking in Hmong. Ms. M. couldn't understand what we said, but sometimes she reached over and rubbed my back or patted my hand when she could see I was getting stressed out.

My dad told me that Mai had been caught at Shoua's house, that she had spent the night in the hospital, and now she was in the juvenile detention center in Saint Paul. They hadn't gone to see her yet, but I was glad she was safe. Then Brian asked me to tell my parents exactly what I had told him. I started with my confusion about being Hmong and American at the same time, and how I was worried that my dad would make me get married. Then I told them about Ku and how I had sneaked out to go to the dance, and how I broke up with him the next day because it felt wrong. I also told them about running away with Mai, and what had happened to her while we were at Shoua's house.

A few times, my dad tried to interrupt, and he seemed really angry, but Brian told him he would have a chance to talk later, and to let me finish talking. I was as honest as I could be. I didn't leave anything out, not even the kissing part, even though I felt really ashamed and embarrassed. I know I disappointed my parents.

After I finished, everyone was quiet. It was scary.

"Is there anything you would like to say, Mr. and Mrs. Vang?" Brian asked.

My mother thanked me for telling the truth, and she said that she believed me. My father was looking down. He seemed mad, but when I looked closer, I could see he was crying and didn't want anyone to see. Finally he looked up.

"Choua," he said, taking a deep breath, "I've already lost Mai and Ger. Please, I don't want to lose you too."

I started to cry. It really touched me. I think my father was telling me that he forgave me, and asking if we could please try again.

Brian told my parents that I should go stay with relatives for a while. He said we needed to get counseling together so we could figure out how we were going to work things out.

At first they were really upset. My father pounded his fist on the desk, and said it was the Americans trying to get into our family business. My mother just cried and said she wanted me to come home with her. I said the same thing.

Brian calmed us all down and said he was sorry, but he didn't have any choice. He said that this was the best thing for all of us. He said we could decide what to do next in a few weeks.

Then he stood up and said, "But for now, this is the way it has to be. I'm going to take Choua with me. We'll meet you back at your house, and Choua can pack up her things. You make some phone calls and figure out where she's going to go."

"I'll stay with Youa," I said quickly. I didn't want to go stay with any of my aunt's and uncles, that's for sure. At least Youa was modern, and she was easy to talk to.

My parents nodded their agreement. I was sure Youa wouldn't mind.

"Remember, this is not a punishment, Choua. Just think of it as a time-out. Time to chill out and figure some things out without all kinds of problems swirling around you."

I nodded my head. It kind of made sense, but I still didn't like it.

Ms. Martinez said, "I'll come along and help you pack your things, Choua."

I nodded. Thank God for Ms. Martinez! I don't know where I'd be right now if it weren't for her.

~~~

Brian drove me to the house. It was about two in the afternoon so everyone was still at school except for the young ones. I realized both Mom and Dad had to take a day off work to come and see me. I felt bad about that. I had caused so much trouble already, and now they were losing their pay too.

Youa was there with the kids, and she rushed over to me and gave me a huge hug when she saw me.

"Oh Choua," she said, "We're all so relieved you're okay. Thank God! We were going crazy with worry. Mom was sure you and Mai were dead."

I didn't realize how much pain I had caused my family. How could I be so selfish?

Then I blurted out, "Youa, is it okay if I come and live with you for a little while? Brian says I need to stay somewhere else until we get stuff worked out."

Youa hugged me tighter. "I would love that, Choua. You know there's not very much room, but we'll figure it out."

I realized how much I loved my sister and I really felt like everything was going to work out.

"How will I get to school?" I asked Youa. She lived in Minneapolis, and there are no buses going to Como. I felt anxious to get back to my day-to-day life, and I didn't want to miss any more school.

"I'll drop you off on my way here each morning," she said. "It's not big deal. We'll just have to leave a little bit earlier, that's all."

Ms. M. stayed in the living room and talked to Youa while I went to pack my bags. Mom brought me an old suitcase and some paper bags. There wasn't much so it just took a few minutes. Brian and my dad were smoking and talking on the front porch. I saw him come in and look at the lock on the door and the bars on the windows.

While we were in the bedroom my mom said to me, "Choua, we both love you so much. I'm sorry we don't have enough time to take care of you and listen to your problems. I will always love you, Choua, and I am going to spend more time with you, okay?"

It felt good to hear that. I wondered why something so terrible had to happen before I could hear those words.

"I love you too, Mom," I said, hugging her. "I'm going to make you proud of me. Don't worry about me because I'm going to be okay. I'll call you tonight, all right? Everything's going to work out. You'll see."

I believed every word I said.

My mother smiled and said in English, "I know, Choua. Everything work out. Love make everything work out."

Youa got her kids packed up and I put my stuff into her trunk. It was strange to see my mom and dad and Ms. Martinez and Brian standing there on the sidewalk as we drove away. I wonder what's going to happen next.

Wednesday, February 21

It was weird going back to school today. It felt like I had lived a whole other life between the last time I was there and today. The weird thing is none of my friends knew what happened to me even though I felt like ten years had passed.

"Where have you been?" Trisha said, rushing up to my locker this morning. "Were you sick?"

"Yeah," asked Bee, joining her. "What's going on? I tried to phone you last night and your sister said you weren't living at home anymore."

The bell had rung, and I was already running late because Youa got caught in traffic on the way to school. I said, "We'll talk at lunch when Frankie's here too. Meet me at my locker, and I'll tell you everything then."

My first class was social studies. I felt sick. What was I going to say to Ku? We always sat together now, but I didn't feel like I could today. I took a few deep breaths as I was walking down the hallway, but I still felt sick. I stopped off in the bathroom because I felt like I might throw up. I could smell cigarette smoke as I walked into a stall, and there were lipstick-covered butts floating in the toilet water. It grossed me out. I flushed the toilet, put the lid down, and sat down, putting my head in my hands.

"What am I going to do?" I thought. "How am I going to get through this?"

Then I remembered. I started going through my backpack, and pulled out this journal that I carry with me everywhere. I turned to January 16 and reread the words,

I, Choua Vang, make the solemn promise that I will make my dreams come true, and I will do what I want to do, and not what others think I should do. I will always follow my heart.

I stared at the words for a long time, and asked myself, "How will you follow your heart? What does that mean? What is your heart telling you to do?"

Then I knew. My heart was telling me to do nothing. For now. Just wait. I decided that I would talk to Youa and see what she thought. But for now there was nothing that I needed to do. I decided I would smile at Ku if our eyes met, but nothing else. It helped that I was coming in late too. There wouldn't be a chance to talk before class, and I'd rush out as soon as class was over.

As it turned out, there was nothing to worry about because Ku wasn't even there. At first I was relieved, but then I felt kind of worried. Was he cutting class? I wonder if he's avoiding me.

I told Frankie and Bee and Trisha everything at lunch. They could hardly believe it. It had been just a normal few days for them, but my life had turned totally upside down. After creative writing this afternoon, I stayed to talk to Ms. M. She told me she'd pick me up and take me for lunch on Saturday, and we could talk then. She's pretty awesome. Between her and Youa and my mom, I feel like there are some great women in my life. I know they'll all help me.

Friday, February 23

I've been at Youa and Tou's place for a few days now. It's kind of strange living with Youa, but it feels good. She takes good care of me. I don't know if Tou's parents were very happy when I showed up at their house, but Youa was very strong and told them that they would just have to get used to it. They live in an old house, and it's full of people. There are four bedrooms: Tou's parents have one, Youa, Tou and the kids have another, Tou's three brothers share another, and his two sisters in elementary school, and sleep in the smallest one. Youa said she wants to move out as soon as they can because there's just not enough room, plus her and Tou really want to get their own place. There's no privacy here.

There's really no room for me except in the basement which is tiny and full of boxes and wet laundry hanging from ropes zigzagging across the ceiling. There's a washing machine down there, but no dryer. Youa found an old foam mattress and some sleeping bags, and we put them down on the hard cement floor. It's cold down here, but I wear my sweater and socks to bed and I manage okay. I turned a box over to use as a nightstand and I have a little lamp that I can read and write with. I use another box to keep my clothes and underwear in, and some stuff is on hangers hanging from the ropes on the low ceiling. I do my homework on my bed, sitting cross legged. It's actually okay, because I get lots of private time and nobody bothers me downstairs.

Youa and I talk a lot. Sometimes she comes down and sits on my bed with me and we drink tea together, and sometimes I hang out in her bedroom with her. Mostly we talk about me and how I'm doing and what I'm thinking. I've been feeling really sad about Ku the last few days. It seems like I've lost so much in such a short time.

Youa told me, "You need to concentrate on your girlfriends, Choua. It sounds like you've got great friends, and you stand by each other. Spend time with them, and try to forget about boys."

"But what should I say to him when I see him in class?" I asked her. He still hasn't shown up and I'm worried.

"Just tell him you're sorry things didn't work out," she said. Then she added, "But tell him when your friends are around. They'll help you feel stronger plus you won't have to be alone with him. I think it's important that you don't spend any more time alone."

I agreed with her, but I still couldn't stop thinking of our kisses.

"That's easy for you to say," I said. "You've got Tou."

"Just remember what happened to me, Choua," Youa said. "Whenever you're tempted to get together with Ku or some other boy, just remember that. There's lots of time to fall in love. Now isn't the time."

"But I'll probably never get to fall in love," I whined. "If Dad makes me get married..."

"Let's just take this one step at a time, baby sister," Youa said. "Mom doesn't think any of you girls should get married until you're out of high school. Maybe she can persuade Dad."

"Did she tell you that?" I asked her, surprised.

"Yeah, and she also said she didn't see what was so wrong with falling in love."

"Wow," was all I could say. It's good to know my mom is on my side. Maybe she'll be able to talk to Dad and help him understand. It must be so hard for them. I mean, they both come from the same culture, but they've been forced to change in so many ways. It seems like my mom has been more willing to change, and my dad is just so determined to hang onto being Hmong that it's turned him bitter and angry. Youa says she remembers him being very kind and laughing a lot when she was a little girl in Thailand. He almost never laughs now. It seems like he's always angry.

"Do you think there's any hope for me, Youa? Do you think I'll be able to go to college and marry the man I want?" I asked her.

Youa reached over and grabbed my hand. "Choua," she said. "Never give up hope. You're strong, and you can make good choices for yourself. I believe that, and I'll help you, I really will."

Who knew I had such a cool sister? I'm so glad to be hanging with her and learning so much.

"You know what else?" she added.

"What?" I asked.

"By the time you graduate in a few years, the kids will be in school. Maybe we can go to college together!"

How cool would that be?

Saturday, February 24

I got up early this morning to help Youa do chores around the house. I hardly talk to anyone around here but her and Tou. I suppose I should make friends with his sisters, but I just don't feel like I have the energy. The girls are very sweet, but they leave me alone. I think they must think I'm some tough gang kid who's going to make them take drugs and steal. That makes me laugh. I'm not tough. I feel like I'm still the same shy little skinny kid I was in Head Start. How can I be almost grown up?

Anyway, I scrubbed the bathroom (gross!) and then helped

vacuum and sweep the floors until it was lunchtime. Then I had a quick shower in the nice, clean tub and put on my jeans and a blue sweater Youa said I could wear. It stank a little like baby puke, but I tried to ignore that.

Ms. Martinez picked me up at around noon and we drove to a Perkins not too far away. I ordered a hamburger and fries, and she had a salad. She told me she was trying to lose weight because her wedding was coming up in a few months.

"I forgot you were getting married," I said. I felt guilty because I had been so busy thinking about myself the last few months, I never even asked her about what's going on in her life. I wonder if all teenagers are this selfish?

"What's your fiancee like?" I asked her. "Is he cute?"

She giggled. "Well, I think he is. That's what's important, right?"

I nodded, and bit into my hamburger. I like Hmong food a lot better than American food, but it's okay for a change.

"What's his job?"

"He works at an employment center, helping African Americans get trained for jobs."

That seemed kind of strange to me. "Why African Americans?" I asked.

Ms. Martinez took a sip of her coffee. "Louis is black," she said.

I set my hamburger down on the plate, and wiped my mouth with a napkin. I didn't quite know what to say or do.

"He's black?" I asked. "I don't get it."

"What is there to get?" she asked. "We met and we fell in love. He's the sweetest, kindest man I've ever met."

None of this made any sense to me, but I felt kind of ashamed, like I should understand better. Was it okay for a white person to marry a black person? I had heard about Hmong women marrying white men, but usually they weren't part of the clan after that. It was like they weren't Hmong anymore.

"But you're not African American," I finally said, even though it sounded bad. "Why would you marry a black person?"

Ms. M. finished eating her salad, and put down her fork. I couldn't tell if she was mad. I was scared that she might be. The last thing on earth I wanted to do was make Ms. Martinez angry at me.

"Choua, there are some things you don't understand yet. I think it's important that we talk about them," she said slowly.

I nodded and picked at my fries, swishing them around in the ketchup.

"Choua, look at me," she said. "Please don't think I'm angry when I tell you these things, okay? I'm not angry at all, but I think you've got some misunderstandings about people, and we need to discuss them, okay?"

"Okay," I said, still not knowing what to think.

"First off," she went on. "I get the feeling that you don't like blacks. Maybe you've had some bad experiences, is that right?"

I nodded my head.

"I want you to think about something," she said. "Do you think people judge you because of the color of your skin or the way you look?"

I thought of all the people over the years who have told me to go back to my ***ing country. "All the time," I answered.

"Do you think black people are judged in the same way?"

"Yeah, I guess so," I said.

"Interesting!" she said. "So you already have something in common with them."

I had never thought of that before.

"And who do you think has the easiest time living in America?"

That was simple. "White people," I answered.

"And why is that?" she asked.

"I don't know," I said slowly. "I guess because there's so many more of them, and they kind of control stuff in America."

"That's right," she said. "White people in America are sometimes called the dominant culture. That means they have a lot of control over how things are run like the government and schools and businesses."

"It shouldn't be like that," I said. "It's not fair."

"No, it isn't," she agreed, "but it's slowly changing. People from other cultures are starting to get some of the power too. We're starting to find our strength and power in this country."

"But I bet the white folks like having all that power," I said. "It must be nice." I thought about how many times I wished I were a white kid growing up in a nice home, always knowing what was going on in class, not having to worry if I didn't look right or didn't know what a word meant or how I was expected to behave.

"Some of them like all that power," she said, "but many of them believe that *all* people are important, and *everyone* should have a say. Many believe we are equal."

"Yeah, but lots don't," I said.

"Do *you* think all people are equal and should be respected and treated the same?" she asked me.

"Of course," I said. I didn't even need to think about that.

"What about African Americans? Do you believe they are as good as you are? Or do you think maybe they're not as smart or they don't deserve to get good grades or to get good jobs?"

I blushed when she said that. I didn't know what to say.

"It's something to think about, isn't it?" she said. "Remember the rule I have in my class? What is it?"

"Treat others the way you want to be treated," I said. I took a deep breath, and then picked up my cold hamburger and took a big bite because I didn't know what else to do. Ms. Martinez didn't say anything. I felt like she was waiting for me.

I finished chewing and said, "I see what you're saying. I never thought about it in that way."

"Prejudice comes from not thinking, Choua. It also comes from ignorance. Why do you think some people hate Hmongs?"

"Because they don't understand why we're here or what we're about!"

"Bull's eye," she said, and her eyes twinkled. "Think the same thing might be true of African Americans?"

"Yeah, I guess so," I answered.

Everyday I deal with prejudice: people judging me because I'm Hmong. I never stopped to think that I was doing the same thing to others.

Before we finished eating Ms. Martinez said, "I want you to meet Louis, Choua. I think you'll really like him."

"I'd like that," I said. Ms. M. gave me a lot to think about today.

Tuesday, February 27

I spent the rest of the weekend thinking about what Ms. M. and I had talked about. I can't believe how blind I've been! I know I write about how I hate black kids all the time, and I never realized that I was being just like the people who treat me so badly. That just blows me away. Why aren't I thinking about important stuff like this all the time? Instead I worry about if my boobs are growing or why I'm not pretty enough and junk like that. I'm going to try and spend more time thinking about serious stuff from now on.

I've actually been thinking about something pretty serious today. Ku and I finally talked. I saw him in the hallway this morning, even though he hadn't been in social studies class for the last three periods. I got that sick feeling in the pit of my stomach as soon as I saw him. I wanted to turn around and sneak away before he saw me, but I remembered who I was, and that I had to be strong. I was just coming from math with Frankie so I said, "Can you wait here for me? I want to talk to Ku."

"Are you sure?" she asked.

I swallowed. "I'm sure," I said. "Just don't go anywhere."

I straightened my shoulders and walked toward him, trying to act confident, even though I felt like a teeny mouse.

"Hi," I said. "I haven't seen you around lately."

He looked confused and scared. "What do you want?" he asked.

That hurt my feelings, but I took a deep breath and said, "Listen, I just wanted to tell you how sorry I am. I really messed up."

His face got kind of red and he shoved his hands in his pocket. I couldn't help thinking how cute he was.

"Yeah, you messed up all right," he said. He stood there for a few seconds and neither of us knew what to say. I remembered how incredible it was when we were kissing, but then I pushed it out of my mind.

"See you around," he said. "I gotta go."

And then he walked away, leaving me standing there in the middle of the hallway, feeling like the loneliest, saddest person on the planet.

Thursday, March 1

My parents and I have been meeting with Brian at the Lao Family Center two times a week. Today was our fourth visit. So far we've mostly talked about how hard it is living in between two cultures, and trying to figure out how we can make it work for our family. I think it's hardest for my dad. He doesn't like to talk about his feelings, plus he's the one who is least willing to change. The last three times he just sat slouched in his seat and refused to say anything. I was feeling pretty discouraged about it because I didn't know how I'd ever be able to come home if he kept acting like that.

But today something happened to change all that. My mom had just finished saying how she thought I should be able to go out and spend time with my friends if I earned their trust back.

My dad looked at her and said in a voice that sounded like he was shooting bullets, "Who cares what you think, woman? I'm the boss. I decide what happens with our children. I'm tired of you trying to turn us into an American family. We're Hmong, and don't ever forget it."

My mother looked hurt, and her eyes filled up with tears.

"Do you have something to say to your husband?" Brian asked my mom.

She looked up and raised her chin. "Yes, I do," she said, and I saw her taking a deep breath like I do when I'm about to do something I'm really scared of. "Husband," she said, "you are destroying our family. Our children hate you. Is it more important that you are a strong Hmong man in charge of his family or is more important to be a good and loving father that your children can look up to and respect?"

My father looked down, and I saw the anger in his eyes turning to sadness.

I was so proud of my mother. She went on, "You said yourself that you have already lost Ger and Mai. If they felt safe and loved in their family, why would they have to go and join gangs? It's not only their fault, Husband. It's our fault too. We need to change or we will lose all of our children. Don't you understand?"

My mother started to cry. I didn't know what to do. I just sat quietly and watched the scene unfold like a movie. I could tell something very important was happening.

There was a long silence. Everybody waited. Finally my father talked.

"You're right," he said. And I knew he meant it. It was only two words, but I know it is the beginning of a different path for our family.

I feel like I can breathe again after holding my breath for a very long time.

Monday, March 5

Today was an awful day. I hate African Americans and I don't care what Ms. Martinez and I talked about the other day.

It happened first thing this morning. I was late again, thanks to Youa and her stupid kids, and I was racing to get to my locker. There were crowds of kids going to first period, and I accidentally bumped into a kid as I rushed by. Just my luck, guess who it was? You guessed it. Leticia.

"Hey, what do you think you're doing?" she said in that huffy, loud voice of hers. "You trying to make me angry, little Hmong girl?"

"Sorry," I said. "It was an accident."

"Oh yeah?" she asked, making like she was bending down to pick up the books she had dropped. Instead, she hit me in the legs and knocked me to the floor. I felt my butt hit the ground hard.

"Hey!" I yelled. "What's the matter with you? I told you it was just an accident."

"Yeah, right!" she yelled. "You just think you're better than me, you little bitch!"

Then she started to punch me. I couldn't believe it. I've never been in a fight in my life. I started to punch back. I had no choice. Our fists were flying, and I felt some terrible pain when her hand connected with my cheek.

How dare she? I've never been so angry. She must weigh twice as much as I do, but I felt like a professional wrestler. I could have killed her. I was swinging and slapping and kicking, and then we were rolling on the floor. I heard someone yell, "Girl fight!" and I knew there were crowds of people around us, but none of it meant anything to me. All I wanted to do was kill that bitch Leticia.

Then I felt big hands on my shoulders, and I looked up and saw the assistant principal. So guess where I got to spend the day? In ISS with an ice pack on my face. I've got a big black eye and bruises all over my body. I can hardly move I'm so stiff. And I'm suspended for three days. I spent today in school, but the next two days I have to stay home. Can you believe it? It wasn't my fault! Now nobody's ever going to trust me again. My life sucks.

Thursday, March 8

I spent the last two days hanging out in the basement at Youa's place. Tou's sisters must really think I'm some kind of dangerous homeboy now. I just don't get it. Every time I mess up, I don't realize it until it's too late and then I've gone and ruined everything. I'm all dressed and ready to go to school, but Youa's still feeding the kid's breakfast. I wish she'd hurry up. I've been late almost every day since staying here. She's got to come in to the office and sign something as my legal guardian before they let me back in school. That's what they do to suspended kids. I wish she'd hurry up.

~~~

It's after school, and I'm wrapped up in my sleeping bag on the basement floor. It feels like a long time ago since I wrote that this morning. This is a day I won't forget in a long time. I guess a lot of my days are like that these days. It's so quiet down here. All I can hear is the furnace starting and stopping, and the washing machine swishing around. At least I can keep my clothes clean here. I wash them all the time.

I hardly know how to explain what happened today so I'll start from the beginning. I don't know how I feel about it yet. Youa finally got me to school, but first period had already started. I was so annoyed with her on the drive to school that I just turned the up radio really loud so we wouldn't have to talk. We walked to the office, and Youa started acting all mother-like. It was so embarrassing! I just sat on a chair in the office and pretended the whole conversation had nothing to do with me. As I was sitting there the social worker walked in.

"Aren't you the girl who got suspended for fighting the other day?" she asked.

"Yeah," I muttered, but I didn't look up. Did everyone know?

"I think you and that girl should have some peer mediation," she said. "You need to talk about what happened or it's going to happen again."

She had to be kidding!

"That's a good idea," Youa said. I wanted to kill her. They wanted me to talk with Leticia and work out our problems? Good luck!

"I'll set you up with one of the senior students who's really good. 12:30 should work. What's that girl's name you got in the fight with?"

"I didn't get into a fight with her," I corrected her. "She got in a fight with me!"

"You see? It sounds like you have some issues to work out. Now what's her name?" she said. God, I hated her.

"Leticia," I said miserably.

"Good, I'll let her know. I'll see you in my office at 12:30. You can get a pass from the secretary."

My day was getting off to a bad start, and let me tell you, I was pissed off! I spent all morning feeling angry and dreading the stupid peer mediation. I didn't even know what peer mediation was, to tell the truth.

12:30 rolled around and instead of going to health class, I said good-bye to my friends (who were feeling really sorry for me!) and walked the long hallway to the social worker's office. Today it seemed especially long.

I knocked on the door and a black girl wearing glasses and overalls answered the door. Her hair was in dreadlocks and was almost as long as Mai's. She was wearing a big cross necklace.

"Hi, I'm Kim," she said. "Mrs. Rapin said we could use her office to do the peer mediation. Leticia should be here in a minute. Have a seat."

"Thanks," I said, and slumped down in a chair. I didn't see how it was going to help having two black girls ganging up on me. I really didn't think we were going to get anything worked out.

Leticia came in a second later, gave me a nasty look, and sat down in the chair furthest away from me.

"All right, you guys," Kim said. "Let me tell you how this works."

We both pretended to ignore her when she talked, but I was listening pretty closely. Basically she told us that we were going to find a way to work out our problem and come up with a plan so it wouldn't happen again. She told us we wouldn't start until we had agreed to a few rules. First, we weren't allowed to have any put downs or threats. I couldn't see how Leticia would be able to control herself. She also said we couldn't interrupt each other, and that we had to talk about our feelings as honestly as we could.

"Do you both agree to that?" she asked.

I nodded and Leticia said, "I guess so."

"Who wants to start by telling what happened?"

"I will," I said. I didn't want Leticia making up any lies before I had a chance to say what really happened.

"Okay, go ahead," Kim said. "And remember Leticia, no interruptions. You can tell your side of the story when Choua's finished."

"Yeah, yeah," Leticia said, but she sat there with her arms crossed over her big boobs, like she wasn't going to let me get away with anything.

It didn't take very long for me to tell my side of the story. I just told exactly what had happened.

"Leticia, would you agree with that?" Kim asked after I finished talking.

No answer.

"Leticia?"

"Yeah, I agree," she said.

You could have knocked me over with a feather, I was so surprised.

"So why'd you try and beat me up then?" I asked. "I don't get it."

She looked at me and shrugged. "You just get on my nerves, I guess."

I got on her nerves? She had to be kidding. First off, she didn't even know me, and second, how could I get on someone's nerves? I just sit quietly in the corner and never bother anyone.

Kim stepped in and said, "Why don't you tell Choua why you feel that way?"

Leticia was leaning forward and looking at Kim. "It's like she's the exact opposite of me," she said.

"Don't talk to me, talk to her," Kim said.

She looked at me and continued, "I mean, you just sit in class so quietly, and never have anything to say. You never bother anyone. You're skinny and pretty, and I'm fat and ugly. You're quiet and sweet, and I'm loud and mean. You're everything that I'm not."

Leticia finished and looked down, like she was embarrassed or something. I was too shocked to say anything.

"Choua, how does that make you feel?" Kim asked.

"I dunno," I answered. "Surprised, I guess."

"How come?"

"Well," I said slowly, "Leticia always gets all the attention." I looked over at her, remembering I was supposed to be having a conversation with her. "I guess I thought that's what you liked."

"I want to be liked," she answered. "Everyone likes you."

"No, they don't!" I said. "I only have three friends in the whole school. That's it!"

"What about that boyfriend of yours?"

"We're finished," I said bitterly. "It's over."

Kim stepped in and said, "How does it make you feel to know that Choua doesn't have many friends, Leticia?"

"At least she doesn't have enemies," she answered.

This wasn't making a whole lot of sense to me, but it actually felt kind of good to be having a heart-to-heart with the girl who's made my life miserable all year.

"I'm gonna tell you something, little Hmong girl, but you can't tell anyone else," Leticia began.

"Jeez, I wish you'd stop calling me that!" I said angrily.

"Oh yeah?" Leticia sat up straight and mean in her chair and became the Leticia I was scared of again.

"Yeah," I said. "I mean, it hurts my feelings. Just call me by my name. I don't call you big black girl, do I?"

That made Leticia laugh. "Okay, okay," she said. "I'll call you—what's your name again—Chew?"

"Chew-a," I corrected her.

"All right, Choua, you promise you ain't gonna tell anyone what I'm gonna tell you?"

"Yeah, all right," I answered.

"Okay, it's like this. My step dad is always beating me up. He's a total bastard. I hate him so much I want to kill him. I used to run to the apartment next door when he got into one of his moods. A Hmong family lives there. The lady was real nice at first. She'd let me in and clean me up, and hide me there until my step dad calmed down."

I was listening carefully.

"So anyway, a few months ago I got beat up real bad, and when I went next door, the Hmong bitch wouldn't let me in. She said it upset her husband and kids too much. So I was crying and saying, "I don't have anywhere else to go; he's gonna kill me," but she just pushed the door shut in my face and double locked it. Me and my mom was on the streets for a week, and then they put me in a group home. Since then, I've been going from place to place. You know, foster homes and shit. My mom comes and visits me, but she's still living on the street."

I could hardly believe what I was hearing. Leticia's life was worse than mine!

"So let me get this straight," I said. "You hate me because I remind you of some Hmong woman who wouldn't protect you from your stepdad?"

"Yeah, I guess that's it," she answered.

Kim stepped in again and asked me what I had to say to that.

I had a lot of stuff I wanted to say and I didn't know quite where to start. "First," I said, "I'm sorry. It sounds like you have a pretty shitty life. When people act like jerks, I never ask myself why they might be acting that way. I mean, it makes me so angry that you're always picking on me, but I guess I kind of understand why now."

Leticia looked at me and nodded.

"Second, I don't think it's very fair that because some Hmong woman screwed you over, you have to treat all Hmong people like they're sacks of shit, especially me. I mean, it's not all Hmong people. It's one person, that's all."

The last thing I had to say was the hardest, but I decided Leticia had been brave enough to tell me what she was thinking so I would tell her.

"Third, I've never liked black kids. They scare me. I've been picked on and beat up by black kids all my life. Plus you all act so different from Hmong kids. So I guess," I said slowly, "the way you've decided not to like Hmong people because of a bad experience is the same way I've been about blacks."

Wow! I couldn't believe I'd figured that out, and that I had the

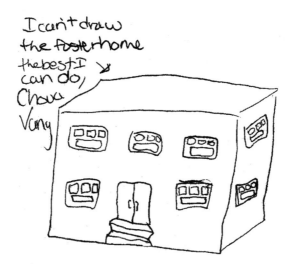

I can't draw
the foster home
the best I
can do,
Chau
Vang

nerves to say it to Leticia's face. I was scared that she might start beating on me again.

"Leticia, do you have something to say?" Kim asked.

"Well, I guess we're both in the same boat. I mean, people treat
us badly because of what they think we stand for. They don't bother
figuring out what we're like on the inside," she said.

I always thought Leticia was kind of stupid, but now I knew she
wasn't. What she said was exactly right.

"It sounds like your life really sucks, Leticia," I said. "I'm real
sorry about that."

Then I told her about Ger and Mai and running away and having
to live with Youa. She was pretty surprised to hear about my life. And
I'll tell you what: by the end of our talk, I think we were pretty close
to being friends. Is that possible? I'm sitting in the cold, wet basement
shivering while I write this. Maybe I just woke up from a dream.

I love ordering a hot fudge sundae and watching the ice cream
push itself away from the hot fudge poured over it. Then when you're
eating it they both come together and slide down your throat in a

trickle of sweetness. Maybe that's what Leticia and I are like. When we actually come together, we're pretty darn good.

I'll say it again: life sure surprises you sometimes.

Tuesday, March 13

I just got some bad news. Mai is out of the juvenile detention center, but she's pregnant. I talked to her on the phone for about half an hour tonight. She's at home, but she's moving out in a few days. When Dad found out she was pregnant, he said she wasn't welcome in the house. He's given her three days to get out.

"Where are you gonna go?" I asked her.

"Mom's phoning around to the relatives for me. I'm getting out of town. I'll probably go to Eau Claire," she said. She sounded pretty calm.

"Aren't you angry?" I asked. "This is horrible."

"No, I'm finished being angry," she answered. "I'm just finished with everything. I just want to get the hell out of Saint Paul and start a new life."

"But what will you do?" I asked her. She sounded so different from the angry, spitting Mai I was used to.

"I thought about getting an abortion," she answered. "That's what Dad wants me to do. But I just can't. I'm gonna quit school. I'm so far behind now anyway that I'll never catch up. I'll probably get a job at Rainbow Foods or something until the baby comes. Then who knows."

"What about the father?" I asked. "Can he help?"

Mai laughed. "Choua, do you think I know who the father is? Don't you remember that everyone has screwed around with me?"

It was one of the saddest telephone conversations I'd ever had. I wished we were together. Then at least I could hug her. Even if she is cold and hard and mean, I would still hug her tonight if I could.

"I wonder if I'll ever see you," I said in a small voice.

"We'll keep in touch," she said. "I'll call you. Maybe you can come and see me in Eau Claire in the summer."

"Yeah, sure," I answered. "That'd be nice."

"Choua, listen to me," Mai said. It sounded like she had got some of her energy back. "Just remember me when you're tempted to go screwing up your life. I'm getting out of the gang now. I can't stay in a gang when I have a baby on the way, can I? But I have to leave home and leave my family. You see? Now I have no family at all."

"You've got me," I said. "I won't desert you."

"Thanks, Sis," she said. "I appreciate that."

There was a kind of embarrassed silence, and then she said, "I gotta go now. Just stay out of trouble. Take care, Sis."

And then she hung up the phone.

So that's that. I feel so sad for her, and I'm angry that Dad is making her move out. I bet Mom fought to let her stay. As usual, Dad wins. I wonder how much things have really changed between the two of them. I'm scared to move home again. I think I like it better in this cold, wet basement. At least I'm not around all that anger all the time. It's only me and my sad thoughts and the washing machine making all those dirty clothes clean again.

Thursday, March 15

Today Trisha and Bee and Frankie and I were sitting in the cafeteria having lunch together. They are the only part of my life that helps me feel normal. Youa has let me hang out with them twice after school since I came to live here, and she said that maybe I can go over to Frankie's for a pajama party next weekend. That's the happy part of my life. It seems like most of this journal is about the sad parts of my life. Maybe that's just because there are so many more sad than happy times. I hope things start getting better. I know I'm supposed to follow my dreams and all that stuff, but I don't feel like I have much energy to do that in between all my worries and all the bad stuff that happens to me.

So there we were, laughing and having a great time, eating our disgusting lunch of cafeteria beef stew and strawberry jello with Kool Whip. Suddenly Bee said, "Don't look now, but here comes Ku."

I almost choked on the jello sliding down my throat. "He's coming to see me?" I thought. I flipped my hair behind my ears and wished I had put on some lip gloss.

By this time, all of us had turned to see, but he wasn't coming to see me at all. He walked right past to the table behind us. He sat down beside Mee Lor, a really pretty girl in ninth grade who rides the same bus I used to. She wears expensive, cool clothes and is always giggling. She's one of those Hmong girls who comes from a modern family.

I heard her giggle, and I made myself look at them again. He was kissing her! She was pushing her face away and saying, "Ku, don't do that here. It's embarrassing!" He was kissing her! On the lips!

"Oh my God," said Trisha. "What a jerk!"

"I can't believe it," Frankie said. "Does he know you're sitting right behind him?"

"Of course he knows!" Trisha said. "That's why he's doing it. He wants to make you jealous, Choua. Just ignore him."

I didn't say anything. I finished eating my jello, took a last sip of Coke, and got up from the table.

"Let's go," I said.

I feel like my heart is breaking, but I'm the one to blame. I broke up with *him*. He can go out with anyone he wants.

"Everything is going to be okay, Choua," I keep telling myself. "Everything is going to be okay."

I'm trying to believe that, but I'm not so sure. I haven't even cried. I think I'm going to go upstairs and talk to Youa. She always helps me feel better. I don't have to get through all of this on my own. It's okay to ask for help. Sometimes I forget that.

Tuesday, March 20

As you know, I've been pretty bummed lately. Today, instead of focusing on all the bad stuff, I'm going to talk about what's good. Here's a list:

- Brian said I could go home in two weeks, and my mom has been calling me every night at Youa's to tell me how excited she is. She told me she's planning a big party for the night I come home, and she's going to make all my favorite foods: *mov nplaum* (sticky rice), *khaub poob* (noodle curry), egg rolls and *nab vam* (a really yummy Hmong dessert) for the celebration.

- Ger has been getting lots better. They moved him to this new place called Sister Kinney where he's learning how to use his legs again. He's still in a wheelchair, but Mom says he can come home soon. She said that Dad is building a wheelchair ramp in front of the house so he can get in and out.

- Mai moved to Eau Claire and she phoned me last week. She says she likes living with my cousin Crystal and her husband. I guess they're quite modern, and they only have two kids. Crystal is studying to be a teacher. Mai is working at an Asian food store and helping out with the kids when Crystal goes to school. It sounds like a really good place for her. I hope it keeps her away from gang kids.

◎ I'm not as bummed about Ku and Mee as I thought I would be. He's cute and all, but he's not really my type anyway. I think I'm over him. Like Frankie said once, "There's lots of fish in the sea." Anyway, I'm not thinking about boys right now. Youa's right. I'll concentrate on my friends and studying hard so I can go to college. I'm going to show everybody what I can do!

◎ Leticia and Frankie and I have been sitting together in math class. Actually, I helped Leticia after class yesterday because she doesn't get decimals. She calls me "Sistah" now and she says kids like us need to stick together. I invited her to go to the international club meeting on Wednesday, and she said she'd think about it.

◎ Frankie, Trisha, Bee and me are all going to the international club party on Saturday afternoon. Youa said it was okay. We're all bringing something to eat from our country. Frankie is bringing *fufu*, which I can't wait to try, and Trisha is bringing a special noodle dish from Vietnam. I'm going to Bee's house after school tomorrow, and we're going to make a big batch of egg rolls. Bee's mom is going to drive me home after we're done.

◎ I've applied to get into a summer program at Lao Community called YEEP. It stands for Youth Education and Employment Program. You get to go on tours of college campuses and meet Hmong college students and talk to them about their lives. You also do community service like volunteer at shelters and stuff. Plus you get paid!

◎ Ms. M. and I are going out again this Sunday. She's taking me to the Mall of America and we're going to have lunch and look around in the stores. I haven't been there in months and months. I can't wait. After that, we're going out for dinner with Louis. I'm going to start going to her house every weekend to work on this book so maybe it will be ready soon. I hope you enjoy reading it and it makes you think a bit. If you can learn from my mistakes, I think that would be really cool.

So you can see that life is okay after all. I just have to start looking for the good stuff. Life is never going to be perfect, but it's what you make of it. I think it's kind of like glasses. You put on one pair and everything is all blurry and out of focus. But when you put on the right pair, suddenly you can see everything clearly and the sun is shining.

TEACHER'S DISCUSSION GUIDE TO THE NOVEL

The following are discussion topics that may help students synthesize the novel, tie it to their own experiences, and create a dialogue that enhances racial and cultural understanding as well as an appreciation and understanding of literature. These topics could also be used as suggested writing assignments.

1. What are some of the situations in this novel you most clearly identify with? What are some of the things you know nothing about?

2. What do you think about the language in this novel such as the swearing and the slang? Do you think it takes away or adds to the novel?

3. Consider how a journal is different from other kinds of writing. How would this novel have changed if it weren't written in a journal format?

4. Why do you think it is important that there be a novel about Hmong teenagers?

5. What do you think about white writers who write books about other cultures? What do you think they have to do in order to make it authentic and effective?

6. Could this book have been about teenagers from other cultures and still addressed similar issues?

7. Discuss some of the things you learned about Hmong culture through the reading of this novel.

8. Compare and contrast your family with Choua's family.

9. Is it realistic to think you might have friends from other races/cultures? How have you or how could you go about starting a friendship like this?

10. What part of Choua's life did you most closely identify with?

11. In your opinion, what were the major themes of Choua's journal? If you were to keep a journal, what would your major themes be?

12. Do you think the Vangs are a typical Hmong family? Why or why not? Are they similar to your family in any way?

13. What do you think Choua's greatest difficulty was? Do you feel like she resolved her problem by the end of the story? Explain.

14. In your opinion, what mistakes did Choua make? What were some of her positive choices?

15. Do you believe, as Choua does, that white people have an easier life than people from other races and cultures? What makes you think so?

16. Describe some similarities between your culture and another. Now describe some of the differences. What could you do to promote a better understanding between cultures?

17. What is the hardest thing about being a teenager for you?